I0626370

Pleasure as a Higher Calling

Easy & Delicious

Spicy Stories of Life, Love, Sensuality, and Lust

SAVANNAH ARIES

Pleasure Press

Copyright © 2017
Published in the United States of America by Pleasure Press

ISBN-13: 978-0-9974843-0-4

*This is dedicated
to the ones I've loved*

Thank You!

*You inspired me to adopt
Pleasure as a Higher Calling.*

Books by Savannah Aries in the
Pleasure as a Higher Calling series:

Waking Up

Easy & Delicious

No Regrets

Contents

Foreword
Page 7

Easy and Delicious
Page 11

He's Perfect
Page 18

It's Just Lunch
Page 34

Professor William
Page 48

The Drive-By
Page 62

The Car with California Plates
Page 70

That Thing!
Page 88

About the Author
Page 105

Foreword

A Higher Calling:
What Savannah has to say about Pleasure

Pleasure. The word alone makes me smile. I love to think about it, write about it and above all, indulge in it. In my stories I share my intimate experiences and thoughts with humor and honesty. I speak for women of a certain age, who, like myself, refuse to give up on fully engaging in life and all its glorious and abundant Pleasures.

Pleasure is a higher calling for me. Deriving Pleasure from common daily activities is paramount to my enjoyment of life. I consider this my sacred mission of Love: to remind myself and others of what is possible for them as well. It's easy and it's delicious. At any given moment, a mere shift of perception, a sidelong gaze toward a more luscious opportunity can be all that's required to savor a sensory experience of beauty or love.

I especially enjoy writing spicy stories about life, love, sensuality and—YES!—lust. I do this for the pure Pleasure that's in it. A life well-lived includes the joy of lovemaking, of great sex, and of course, much more. Living my life as authentically and genuinely as possible is my first Pleasure. Giving my heart, sharing my affection, indulging my senses, enjoying the blessings afforded me—this is my calling. For me this includes delicious food and the Pleasure of preparing it with or for someone I love to dine with. It includes the joy of moving my body with freedom and grace, dancing, stretching, breathing, playing, making love—this is my calling. To express myself colorfully in words, song, activities and celebrations, to create and share that which calls to my soul—this is my calling.

My consideration of Pleasure is interwoven into every worthwhile endeavor. Why devote an ounce of energy to anything else? Pleasure or even the visceral memory of a pleasurable moment can serve to overcome a difficulty both physically and mentally, emotionally and spiritually. Life without a delicious daily dose of Pleasure would be grim indeed.

I'm not naive. Naturally there are certain tasks or situations that don't evoke thoughts of Pleasure. But even nestled within these challenges, is there not inherent in the action of overcoming them, the hopeful desire for an outcome of relief, of a wee bit of Pleasure? Otherwise, how could anyone continue? I practice the discipline of delayed gratification with minimal patience as a coping mechanism when I'm forced to wait for a Pleasure.

Each of us is graced with the choice of how we will respond or react to the hand of fate. No one is spared difficulty. For me, returning my focus to what brings me Pleasure is the antidote to despair. Living a life filled with Pleasure is my desire and sharing it makes life worthwhile. Writing about Pleasure is easy and delicious.

The Spicy Stories

*"One cannot think well,
love well, or sleep well,
if one has not dined well."*
~ *Virginia Woolf*

Easy and Delicious

W andering through my favorite neighborhood market I'm unable to decide what to buy for dinner tonight. Hoping for a suggestion, I stop before our proud Italian butcher's counter and stare into his smudgeless glass display case. Lorenzo loves the Pacific Northwest but he likes to pretend he's still hovering over his open air meat market back home in Sicily. With artistic flair, he stocks and arranges fresh raw hunks of flesh, but nothing captures my imagination.

I text my lover with a request. "What do u feel like eating 2 nite? Something EZ & delish plez."

He texts me back right away. "When I think of EZ & delish, I think of u." He's charming and his flattery coaxes a smile, but right now I need direction. I stroll over to the produce section with the same lack of inspiration. He calls me then. "Let's grill some beef and veggie skewers. Pick up something sweet, like you, for later."

Hearing his playful voice invokes a tingle deep inside. My mind wanders back to last weekend when he was seated across from me. The table was set beautifully with colorful mats and napkins, flickering candles and plates of homemade pasta drenched in fragrant fresh basil pesto that we had spent the afternoon cooking together.

As my mind returns from its seductive reverie to the grocery, my enthusiasm is revived. The colors and textures of vegetables brighten before me. Gently gliding my fingers over the smooth skin of the sweet bell peppers and juicy tomatoes, I notice a zucchini begging me to pick it up. An avocado beckons to me, promising to melt in my mouth. All of these are coming home with me.

Back at the meat counter, Lorenzo can't restrain himself from flirting. "Savannah, so beautiful. Tonight more than ever. What your sexy green eyes wish to see? What I can select for you?" His seductive Italian accent and erotic gestures toward the morsels of meat lining his display case make me blush.

"This sweet lamb. Just for you. So succulent and tender."

"Beef for kabobs?" I ask him, surprised by a sudden shyness.

"You want beef? These filets will satisfy the appetite of lovers. Firm and juicy."

"Perfect, Lorenzo. Max will be pleased." With the proper Latin enticement, shopping for our meal just became the easy pleasure I was hoping for.

Max and I are falling in love. Our friendship is in gestation. We're weekend lovers due to impossibly busy work days, and we're okay with that for now. When we met we knew instantly that we'd make a good match. That first kiss encouraged us to explore our possibilities. We merged and neither of us feels a need to define it. From that moment, nothing on the weekend has mattered more than kissing, talking, touching and making love. Add to that, cooking and feasting on delicious meals, and it's easy to fathom why we rarely venture more than 20 feet from the bedroom or kitchen. Our most voracious appetites are gratified within that radius.

I call him back now. "I'm in the sweets aisle at the moment eyeing some creamy lick-it-off-my-fingers-or-anywhere-you-like chocolate. How does that sound?"

"Damn it woman! I'm in heavy traffic. Licking chocolate off you anywhere? Don't you realize what you do to me when you talk like that? You've created a throbbing road hazard. I nearly swerved into that semi next to me. Save some of that sweet stuff for me, I'll be there in 20 minutes." He laughs and hangs up on me.

This is exactly why standing in the market, deciding what to purchase for a sumptuous meal, is so important. I think about how much we enjoy selecting and preparing our meal together. The delicious flavors and aromas of our foods not only satisfy our bellies but seduce us to experience our ravenous hunger for each other in every way.

I gaze at the chocolat pot de crème and imagine the two of us dipping our fingers into it. The image of Max with a glorious erection blazes across my mind. A visceral memory of him moving inside of me makes me shiver, eliciting an orgasm that ripples throughout my core. The surprise of it threatens to buckle my knees and I cling to the cart for support. We're quite a pair. The mere mention of licking rich chocolate off our fingers makes him stiff and me juicy.

When he arrives, he sets his backpack inside the door and pulls me into his arms. "Come here. Let me hold you. I've missed you all week." He kisses my lips and nibbles on my neck. "You look good enough to eat tonight." His eyes twinkle as he tastes me and I know he means it.

"I hope you're hungry, lover." I melt my body into his.

He walks in the door after a few days away and we start like this. We kiss and the world slows down to one breath. We gaze longingly into each other's eyes, knowing smiles slowly sneaking across our faces. The kiss becomes soft and searching. My breath catches. I pull him closer, nuzzling into his chest. We linger at the door a moment longer. Then he takes my hand and leads me into my bedroom to cuddle, kiss and catch up from our days apart.

I like to sample a morsel of his earlobe and run my fingers through his cropped silvery crew, massaging his scalp to dissolve the tension and stress of his day at work. Max sets about to rediscover my body every weekend. He pulls off my shirt burying his face in my breasts.

"Max, I've missed you so much. When I was choosing our treat at the market earlier, I was rocked by the yummiest orgasm just thinking about you for dessert."

His deep brown eyes shine with amusement while he unzips my jeans and peels them off. "This right here is what I think about all week, darlin." His middle finger strokes me through my silk thong. "Earlier today I was in a slump with a deadline to meet and nothing creative coming to mind. I closed my eyes and imagined your sexy smile. How smooth and warm your skin feels. The way these silky blonde strands of hair fall across your face as you turn to reach for me. The thought of making love to you inspired me. Your lips and tits and this little bud right here are an aphrodisiac that fans my creative fires."

His confession moves me like an unexpected answered prayer. He whispers these endearments as his mouth searches for and finds each secretly yearning crevice of my body. He samples bits of me as if I were a luscious hors d'oeuvre. I could dine out forever on just his kisses, but when he moves inside of me I'm insatiable. Our lovemaking is an aperitif that whets our appetites till we're ready to get up to make dinner.

Max digs into his backpack and produces a lovely bottle of Chianti, opening it with a flourish. He laughs when I tell him that Lorenzo would approve. He pours, we toast and take a sip. It's good. Now he's ready to assemble the beef and veggie kabobs marinating in olive oil, garlic, fresh herbs and spices.

"This is top quality beef. Tell Lorenzo I'm impressed."

"The grill?" I ask with dread. It's so cold out tonight.

"No. Not tonight, darlin."

Thank God. Barefoot in his T-shirt and boxers and my only cover a large chef's apron, I'm relieved. He loves to grill and is usually not so easily dissuaded from the idea, even in the dark and rain. But tonight he's content to arrange his colorful stick designs artfully on a cast iron rack to broil in the oven instead.

I blend a lemony avocado dressing with a hint of summer savory, the last of this year's garden, and toss it onto our organic butter leaf salad. He pulls apart a warmed baguette and slathers it with French triple cream butter. Our simple meal is prepared and we are ready to indulge.

We dine slowly and sensuously by fingers and candlelight, taking time to savor the flavors, colors, textures and each other. We're new, so our dinner conversation trends to stories of our past, our interests, our hopes, our thoughts and feelings about the world we live in.

But we don't share everything. I've had experiences, heartaches, and disappointments I'd rather he didn't know about. Not yet. He's been a soldier. We haven't broached that. The world we are creating together now is sheltered and private. We enjoy each other. That's enough.

After a while, Max clears the table, leaving the dishes in the sink. Yawning, he says, "The night is but a pup, darlin'. Let's grab a little nap."

I laugh because even though we may both feel like a nap, we haven't been able to manage one yet, no matter how exhausted we are. The minute we lay down, the twinning of our bodies, the touch of warm skin each to the other, excites an irresistible urge to delve ever deeper into one another's essence. The dreamy, almost effortless way we engage requires surprisingly little aerobic activity. We can make love for hours.

All week I yearn for the way his lips and tongue nibble and suck and hunger for me. I revel in the potent orgasms he elicits, evocative waves rolling in and crashing over me. He's as dedicated to my continuing pleasure as I am to his.

When I touch him he completely surrenders to the exploration of my hands and mouth. I have gone on journeys to his most secret sensual places. I love the way he holds his breath, releasing into deep sighs of pleasure as I lightly drag my fingers down his back or across his chest. When I kiss his cheek or slide my lips to his ear lobe, he stills himself and receives me before seeking my lips to kiss in return.

An intrinsic component to our sustained lovemaking is this man's sensitivity to me. That, and his undaunted staying power. Oh God. He chuckles when I ask him if he's trained in Tantra. He has the ability to experience orgasm without ejaculating. Not until he senses that I am completely satisfied, not until we are ready to climax one last time together does he allow himself to come inside of me. He knows exactly when the perfect last minute has arrived.

As I perch atop him he matches my movements slowly and deliberately. He senses what I desire and gives it to me. When he knows we're ready, he rolls me onto my back, positioning himself over me. I guide his firm eager cock back into my slippery opening. We're a perfect fit. I move with him, for him, because of him.

Max watches me, gauging to see how far he can take me. When he erupts into me, it's volcanic. Did I think I was spent? I'm mistaken. I reverberate with the powerful energy we generate together and contract around him in waves of ecstasy again. We take each other to that place every time.

When we're completely overcome, we lay curled together in bliss. Just before drifting off to sleep I remember the chocolate dessert. "Max, sweetheart, I promised you something. Something sweet, creamy and delicious."

"And I bless you," he answers dreamily. His eyes are closed. He is still far away. I wait a few more minutes for him to rein himself in, letting the idea of our dessert sink into his imagination, rouse him from his reverie.

I sense he needs an encouraging reminder. "There's chocolat pot de crème," I whisper. "There's fingers meant to double dip," I giggle. "There's cool creamy chocolate waiting to be slathered and licked from delectable places." I tremble in anticipation.

"Mmmm." He opens his eyes and kisses my cheek. "Let's do it."

"Yummy," we coo in chorus. Naked in the kitchen in the middle of the night, we suck each other's chocolaty fingers. He paints designs on my belly button and nipples. I draw a thick curled mustache on the sides of his penis. Smeared with chocolate, our mouths lick our sticky creations. It's a good night about to become an even better morning.

Max runs a soft cloth under warm water, and lovingly tidies me up. I return the favor before we slip back into bed. We are lovers with lusty appetites. But in this divine moment, we are all each other wants or needs. Our longing to indulge in and savor our coupling is complete, for now. As I lie wrapped in his arms, his warmth penetrates me, comforts me and lulls me to sleep. I know we are blessed. This is how we entertain ourselves on the weekends. Making love with interludes of easy and delicious meals takes precedence over any other well-intended plans.

Max and I are falling in love.

"The time I burned my guitar it was like a sacrifice.
You sacrifice the things you love.
I love my guitar."
   ~ Jimi Hendrix

He's Perfect

That handsome lead guitar player up there on stage, the one slinging those obscure songs, has captured my full attention. I've heard him once before and both times now he's sung my memory-making favorites. He has presence and his soulful, almost tortured, expressions only add to the turn-on. I brought my buddy Ben along with me to check out the show for a story I'm thinking about writing. But my initial interest in him as a story has shifted. Seeing and hearing him play like that is stirring up something deep within me. My body has joined my mind's curiosity.

When I point him out to Ben and ask what he knows about him, he responds with exaggerated disgust, "Forget him."

"Why?"

"A pile of reasons."

"Like?"

"He's in the middle of a divorce for starters."

"Perfect."

"No, he isn't. Far from it."

"Is he emotionally unavailable?"

"What do you think?"

"Is he hopelessly self-absorbed?"

"Isn't that obvious?"

"Does he think he's God and is he also younger than me?"

"Yes. Jesus, Savannah. Stop!"

"He's perfect!"

"Forget it. He's a mess. Get a life."

"He's perfect for me at the moment." Can't Ben see that my patterns are titillated, my issues are mesmerized, and my angst is on fire? Ben must sense that energy.

"You're a mess. I thought we came here for a story. Grow up. Oh yeah, I forgot. You're getting close to ancient, and yet you still act like some teenage groupie. What does messing with him get you, anyway?"

Ben won't admit it, but he's empathic. I knew he could feel me even though he loathes being so sensitive. "More adventures? More fun? More sex? Don't worry about me. When was the last time you were thoughtfully and thoroughly laid by the perfect mess? They have a certain charm all their own you know, in case you've forgotten." I enjoy rubbing Ben the wrong way.

"Of course I know that. It's the story of my life." We laugh. Ben and I like to one up each other with our battle scars of love. He's become cautious. I haven't.

"You're hopeless," he sighed.

"Not true. I'm always hopeful. Hope is what initiates the story for me. What happens next isn't the important part. Speculating on all the pleasurable possibilities of how a story could play out is what makes it interesting."

"Why are we friends?" Scanning the room for women, Ben nudged me out of his way.

"What's his name, Ben?"

"I refuse to encourage your demise, Savannah."

"I don't need your encouragement. Just introduce me to that guy and I will eloquently orchestrate my own demise . . . with his assistance . . . if I still have what it takes."

"You need help."

"Yes, I do. Come on Benny, help me with an introduction, your responsibility ends there. The fates will manage the rest."

I'm fairly confident that I know this guy's type. He's the kind of guy that women secretly lust for but won't admit it. It doesn't matter that he isn't even close to being in their best interests. Women will ignore that he's good for nothing but heartache and still fall for him. I'm steeped in all that angst and disappointment so I recognize this guy's a perfect match for what I'm interested in at the moment.

"What's so perfect about him? He's fucked up. What do you want?"

"Damn Ben, I'm not planning to marry him. I'm merely interested in a possibility. What if I could get a great interview and also have some fun?" And what if I could untangle some of my ingrained patterns all at the same time? I'd like to discover whether or not my life really is one long Groundhog Day when it comes to men.

"How does hooking up with this loser do anything useful for you?"

"Hey, he poses a challenge worthy of my effort. He's got that look. He plays his guitar like a lover, and his voice gets into me. He's got that something. I plan to write about that. It's why we're here, remember? But now that I've heard him sing those songs and play the guitar like that again, doing that something has become what interests me most tonight." I'm sure I can avoid getting lost in it. The pattern has a possibility of changing by me not getting hooked and not falling for him. It's a gamble I'm ready and willing to take.

"God, you're so arrogant."

"So is he. It's perfect. Anyway, maybe he isn't a loser just because you think he is."

"You're wrong about that, trust me."

"Sweetie, I may trust you, but tonight as you can see, I'm ignoring you."

"Sick and wrong."

"Also bring-on-the-grins fun. I'm smiling right now just thinking about a couple delicious possibilities."

"That puts you on par with him then, doesn't it." Now Ben is bored. He'll wander away soon.

"Guess so. And so what? You guys act like this all the time."

"You're pathetic, Savannah."

"I'm undaunted by your pessimism."

"You're already on the verge of getting lost."

"Ben, don't you get it? That's what makes life an adventure, at least mine. I'm studying this map, trying to decide which way to go. But I can't be sure that where I'm headed is where I'll end up with all those dangerous slippery curves ahead. Don't you think I have what it takes to overcome this challenge? Introduce me to him."

"Savannah, think this over. Write the story and forget the rest."

"Sorry. That's not on my agenda tonight."

The show ended and my so-called friend refused to participate in my demise, so I had to consider how I would orchestrate my own move. It's completely natural for me to extend myself when it comes to something, or someone I'm interested in. That song slinger up there may have a few secrets or a couple minor details I'm not aware of, but I can bet against the house that I already know the gist of his story.

And Ben is right. I'm unrealistically confident about this stuff most of the time. I'll be the first to admit that particular flaw of mine has landed me in plenty of trouble. But tonight, that's not a problem. This story has a built-in ending and by tomorrow it will have written itself.

To get this guy's attention, I can't act like I know the rules of his game. Guys who live a public life on a stage usually need to feel in charge, admired, and generally have entitlement issues. Women like me they avoid. I've had enough experience to recognize when men don't like what they see in my reflection.

If I mirror back to him the façade he has established, the superficial rock star that's plain to see, he'll turn and walk away. If I reveal that I can sense his vulnerability, can touch his sensitivity, he'll turn and run.

He might have something more to offer than what I'll settle for tonight, but that could take some excavating. There won't be time for that. Anyway, I'm looking for a story. If I can straighten out a couple of my issues and still have some fun, it will be time well spent.

"You're too easy," Ben sighed.

"I may be easy but not in the sense that most men prefer."

"And what, exactly, do most men prefer according to you?"

"It's been my experience that most men consider a woman easy if they can get over on her, you know, take advantage of her, get what they want, then drop and forget her, no hassle."

"But you are easy," Ben laughed.

"True, I'm often mistaken for one of those women, at first anyway. But when it comes to the irresistible pleasures of sensuality, I can be easy to catch, not so easy to throw back unless it's what I want too. There's always the question of who has control of the net." I laughed at my clever analogy.

"You really think you have this whole game down, don't you?"

"Hey, you of all people know that I can meet men on their own turf ready to play. Unfortunately, when they discover that I don't care about their rules they usually bolt. You're one of my closest friends and even you think I'm a hassle."

"That you are."

"Ah, but Benny, there have been those rare instances when I've come upon a self-aware man, a secure man who knows who he is and appreciates being recognized by someone who can authentically meet him there." Those scarce instances are raw and ravishing, a win-win encounter, and a chance.

"I'll admit that particular possibility is always on the back of my mind. I'll also admit up front this is not a common occurrence for me and from what I've been told, not so much for men either. Whatever. Tonight I'm on familiar turf."

"And you're on your own."

"Yup."

"I'm outta here." Ben hugged me, then punched my arm. "Be cool."

"See ya." I watched him head toward the exit, stopping to flirt for a minute with a girl at the door who looked a little like his ex. I laughed to myself. His patterns could use some polishing too.

That song slinger commands the stage and he may be a player but I bet he's also insecure. I have no doubt that if I talk to him right, he'll hand over what I'm looking for tonight. What is that exactly? The prospect of mining his musical world for an interesting article my editor can use is quite appealing. And now the possibility of some carnal pleasure for a few yummy hours is even more so.

He's been watching me too and I can sense that he is acutely aware of my focused attention on him during this last set. Even now as he unplugs, winds up cords, takes down his mic and cases his guitar, he's trying not to acknowledge me.

But this is how it is; I know that. I see him smiling to himself. He's probably thinking: she's an easy one . . . no effort required on my part . . . she'll do for tonight. He sees me smiling too. Does he have any idea why? Ha! Let's get this started, rock star.

He has his back to me as I sidle up close alongside him. "Hi. Got a minute? I just wanted to tell you how much I loved your renditions and delivery of some of the best songs ever written." He turns his head and half smiles, his leer a practiced slow sweep up my legs and over my body. I hold my ground. "I wondered if you would consider answering a few questions about your art and craft for an article I'm writing."

He faces me and steps a little too close. I double my grounding. "You're writing an article?" He sneers, "Pretending to be the press isn't exactly a new approach."

This is going to be more fun than I anticipated. "Occasionally I write for a local arts and entertainment rag. I'm not commissioned for this one, but I know they'll run the story if you'll show me some love I can write home about." I flashed him my warmest sexiest smile, casually placed my hand on my hip and subtly tilted it forward to establish my intention. Stifling a giggle, I leisurely tossed my hair back and cocked my head waiting for his answer. I make a convincing groupie.

"You're a fucking whiplash in the making, aren't you? Whatever. What do you want to know?"

He's cute, and he's already on alert. He's perfect. I'm going to make sure it gets hard for him not to participate. "Let's start at the beginning. What's your name, super star?"

"Let's keep this real," he snarled. "Show me your press pass. Are you worth my time or are you full of crap?"

"Whoa! A hostile takeover! Obviously I'll need your name for the article. Let's back up and make this a little more user-friendly." I softened my stance toward him and extended my hand to shake. "Hi, my name is Savannah. But you can check that fact right here on this press pass I'm pulling out of my pocket, just to ease your skepticism." He glanced at it and stepped closer, his intimidating glare like a force field. I fought the visceral impulse to step back from him and amped-up my grounding. "I'm for real, dude. Now it's your turn, handsome rock star. What's your name, and what's most important to you?"

"What's important to me is not wasting my time, Savannah the journalist, if that's what you are."

"I wouldn't be wasting my time if I didn't think you and your story were worth every intriguing minute of it. I'll remember everything you say that matters. I've taken a personal interest in your band and especially you. I intend to write you up right. I think you'll be pleased. What's your name and what should I know about you?" That I haven't already figured out, that is.

He looked me over from head to foot, then peered into my eyes for a second. A slow grin spread across his mouth not quite make it to his eyes. "Fine," he said at last. "We can talk for a couple minutes, but first I need to finish loading up. Won't take long." I stepped to the side of him and leaned toward his guitar, compelled to take a closer look. When I glanced up at him again, his smile had found his eyes. "Tell me where you'd like to have a drink and I'll meet you there," he said.

"Let me help you, stranger, then we can stroll down the street to some little pub, and I'll write every word you say on a napkin."

"Hey, call me Rick, okay?" He said, finally extending his hand to shake mine. "Why be strangers?"

I took his hand and held it warmly in both of mine. "That's my thought exactly, Rick."

"Oh yeah?"

"Yeah." This is fun.

"What do you mean?" His smile slowly left his eyes again.

"I mean I'm ready to learn every important thing about you. We could even jump on a fast train and become close friends." He placed his other hand over mine. His half smile skeptically inched its way back into his eyes. "Where are we hauling this magic music-making stuff?" I laughed.

Then he laughed too, dissipating the tension between us. His body relaxed as he retrieved his hands from mine. Still chuckling, he picked up a cord and handed it to me. Looks like he's decided to come out and play. Off stage, out of the spotlight, he's a little less formidable but much more handsome. I'm guessing he feels protective of—maybe even naked without—his guitar. I'm going to pick up his case and see how he reacts.

"Hey, I'll carry that," he insisted. "It's heavy and it's precious cargo."

"I think I can do it, Rick. I'll be ultra-careful with it."

"No. I'll handle that, thanks anyway. You take these cords."

Yup, there's a back story here that he won't be telling me. I can feel it. He's in the middle of a divorce because his love for his guitar and music are more important than his marriage. She didn't appreciate his genius. He never invited her to his private party. She figured out that the guy she fell for only exists on stage. He couldn't handle her expectations. She couldn't hide her disappointment.

He was disappointed she didn't honor the sacrifices he'd made for his craft. She got tired as hell of hearing about it all the time. He'd always needed time to be alone with his music and she knew that from the start. She signed on anyway, then went to work on him like a damn remodeling project. He resented her for not understanding the depth of his passion. She resented him more for not validating her importance in his life. He got his validation by sleeping with other women. She was heartbroken when she found out, lawyered-up and said fuck you. He's got no space in his world for anyone else right now. He's perfect.

"Hey, are you ready to tell me everything, Rick? Let's walk down to that worn out bar over there. A little table in a dark corner, a shot of tequila and a bunch of napkins is all we need to get this thing started."

"Some tequila sounds damn good about now. Tell you everything? Not likely, though I might admire your persistence."

"I intend to give this story all I've got."

"That a promise?"

"Yes, it is. I'll lay down the most flattering and informative article about Rick the Rock Star, you've ever read. That's my promise to you." I think this is going well. I might even get him to loosen up. We're half way there.

"Ready, Ms. Journalist?"

"Yes I am." Always.

This joint is perfect for us. Obviously many ill-fated romances have originated right here. After a requisite number of tequila shots, and some sloppy suggestive juke box dances, of course. There's that little table in a dark corner, and it's a booth. What more could we ask for? "Okay, handsome rock star, tell me everything I need to know about you. Let's start from the beginning."

"Let's get some shots on the table first, gorgeous."

"Gorgeous? Well, that's very flattering, Rick, but then I couldn't help noticing the heat from your thigh pressing against mine." I feel my bravado returning. "And then there's your not-so-subtle sniff of my hair and neck. Is this where you wish to begin then?" Works for me. He didn't pull away, but I can feel his edge tinged with a bit of antagonism. I might need to lighten up.

"Let's just get this alleged interview underway," he growled.

"Yup, let's just do it." I waved at the bartender. "Hey, barkeep, we'll be wanting a couple shots of tequila off your top shelf right here, right now. Make those doubles, hold the salt, bring some limes and a pile of napkins." Some good smooth tequila should keep this story heading in the right direction.

"I see you know your way around a bar. Top shelf doubles work just fine for me."

The bartender delivers the interviewing supplies to our little table with a conspiratorial grin. The rock star and I click our shot glasses, holding each other's gaze like a dare, before we knock them back. In tandem, we make the same grimacing shot-of-tequila face and laugh. Some drunken fool staggers over from the bar and loads the jukebox with coins, then wanders off to the john, forgetting to select his tunes. We turn to each other, tap our glasses again and finish them off. It's a good start.

"Hey music man, that box is primed and calling out for you to choose the best songs it has to offer. I feel I can trust you with that task. Would you kindly go and stack some, if they have anything decent?"

"Woman, you might just get it about me. My pleasure to be at your service."

"That's all I ask."

"Huh?"

"The pleasure of your . . . uh . . . service." I offer him my most demure smile.

"Right," he says warily, searching my eyes for a second, then turns and saunters over to the jukebox. I watch the way he moves and bends over the box, assessing the way his ass looks from here. Yummy.

"Hey, not a bad selection for a dive like this," he turns and calls to me. "I don't know about you, but I found a few that I wouldn't mind hearing. Let's see if you know this one." The box lights up and his selection begins to play loudly. The sound is surprisingly good, considering.

"Amos Lee's 'Soul Suckers'? In fact I do know this one. Perfect choice, Rick. I really love the way this song moves through the changes."

I knew it. Of course, he's innately got it when it comes to feeling music. But I doubt he realizes that this song is a great set-up. The lyrics are perfect to get him to talk about the more harsh aspects of being in the business of making and selling music, or selling out. I wonder how he feels about the spotlight, his story of fame, to the degree that he's found any.

"Yeah, I dig those changes too and that great lyric: 'Nothing is more powerful than beauty in a wicked world, play it girl'. I've got a feeling you know something about how that plays, don't you?"

"Possibly. I know it's a wicked world. Tell me what moves you to select a song? What made you choose this one? What is it about a lyric that hooks you? Who influenced you the most musically? Do you compose? How would you describe your style? What do you regret the most? To whom are you most indebted? When did you first know you were an artist? How did you decide on your genre? Why the guitar? How many bands have you played with? Who do you wish you could have met and riffed with? How do you hear your music? Are you happy? What disappoints you? What do you want the most?"

"Jesus God!"

"Is that who you call on for inspiration?"

"Christ. Give me a minute, or a month. You just asked me my whole life. Let's order up another round. I need to wrap my mind around your torrent of questions or else clear it. Heavy lifting. Damn." His focus narrowed to his empty shot glass.

"Barkeep, two more like the last, and fast." I shouted as the song ended. "But you take your thoughtful time, rock star. I've got a stack of napkins and the rest of the night to devote to you and your story."

I wonder what I would do if someone asked me a string of loaded personal questions like that. They flew out of my mouth without thinking. Now I'll have to wait and see what he offers of himself. We just shifted into high gear. It feels like we're already screeching around that slippery curve on two wheels, about to careen into a couple different possibilities here. He could freak, go all superficial rock star and just tell me what he thinks will make a good story. Or, he could answer those questions from his soul and give me something worth writing about.

The first possibility is most likely and means we'll get drunk and head straight to his hotel room. The second is more dangerous for both of us. He'll have to consider how much he can trust me with his tenderness, which will challenge my soft spot and core patterns. In the unlikely event that he opens up like that, I'll need to garner enough dominion over myself to fall in groupie love for tonight only. If he does, the story could be great. If I do, well, at least it could be a partial victory, but I'm on shaky ground right out of the gate. Damn it to hell.

The bartender returns with a smirk and another round. "Put those on a tab for me, dude. Ok, Miss Whoever-You-Are, let's even out the playing field with these cactus nectars. Here's to your intrusive inquisitive mind."

"Thank you, and I'll toast you and your best choice of the possibilities laying on this little table here." I hope you choose the authentic one, rock star, but it's your choice.

"What the hell does that mean?"

"All I mean is that we've got a stack of napkins here to either fill with rock star notes or not, depending on which way you choose to go with this interview."

"Is this really an interview?"

"Yes. It was meant to be, or it can turn into something else entirely. Which way you heading, super star?"

"Listen. I can't answer all those heady questions off the cuff."

"Or, you could."

"Or, they could take some reflection."

"Or, they could be answered with your first impulse and then, upon reflection, you could add more richness and depth at the next interview."

"I won't be in town long enough for a next interview."

"Then the interviews could run simultaneously, right now."

"Goddamn you're persistent."

"I can be when I really want something."

"Tell me…exactly what do you want?"

"Enlightenment."

"Jesus."

"I've tried him."

"You have a damn sassy comeback for everything, don't you? Okay, let's get on with it. What's the first thing you asked me?"

"Just start wherever you want. Those inquiries came out in a stream of consciousness and not in any order of importance, necessarily."

"Okay. Songs, lyrics, hooks. That one, by Amos Lee, exemplifies what draws me to do a song. It affects me. The unusual changes from major to minor are the hook for me. The way you reacted to that jukebox choice, confirmed to me that you like this genre and style and since you're coming on to me, I must be on the right track." Rick chuckled and moved a little closer.

"So you choose your material by the way women come on to you?"

"No, I only choose songs for women with green eyes and freckles on their nose like you. Hey, if you're paying attention, the lyrics of the songs I choose are clues that could answer most of your questions." He curved his arm around my shoulders.

"How cryptic, a man of puzzles and mysteries." Damn it. I like him more than I thought I would, which should put me on red alert right now. I don't know why I always end up tempting fate like this. His eyes are beautiful, sensitive and expressive blue. I like the way he feels next to me. I'd like to plunge my hand into his crotch right now and get a feel for the rest of his talents.

"Yeah, it's funny thing about top shelf tequila," he chuckled. "It makes your mind twinkle and everything, even intense personal questions from a smart-ass journalist, seem acceptable."

"Yup, tequila has a delicious way of providing profound clarity and reckless courage," I add. "But before there's too much wreckage from your hand sliding up my thigh and your arm lassoing my shoulder, maybe you could tell me more. Guitars?"

"You're funny, Savannah. Hey, you must know that your thigh sent out some kind of code. What could I do but comply?"

"So you read code too. You have an array of interesting and eclectic talents. Tell me about guitars before I forget why I care."

"Okay, guitars. The first time I picked one up I was about 12. That old Martin molded itself into my hands and melted into my body. That's something I'll never forget. I taught myself some chords and they resonated deep, felt natural, familiar. Haven't put one down for long since." He leaned in even closer. "How do you feel about another round of this tasty cactus contentment?"

"Want me to order, or do you feel like taking command?"

"You seem comfortable in the role of commander, little woman, but I'll take over from here." He waved at our supplier. "Dude. Bring another round of nirvana."

"Hmmm, now you're calling me little woman. You might want to rethink that. But let's continue on. As you can see, I'm honing my chops as a professional journalist by recording your pithy comments on these damp napkins. Ok, so why the guitar and not a piano or bass or horn?"

"I love the tone, the feel, the blend of sound both electric and acoustic. I fell in love, end of story."

"That's a truly passionate love story, and a sweet segue. I dig the way you incorporate the pedal steel. You like the slide, I can tell by your choice of songs the time I heard you before. Tonight you were mostly rocking. Was that a Strat you were making love to high up there on your staged precipice?"

"You do have an unusual way with of expressing yourself, Miss Writer Woman. Yeah, she's my Fender Stratocaster, guaranteed to come every time I play her."

"Do you need a little bump, like Jimi, to ease into her and make her moan that way?"

"What the hell? How do you know what Hendrix played or how and why? Damn."

"Why wouldn't I? So was he one of your main influences, the one you wish you could have met and riffed with?"

"One of the greats, yeah."

"Who else?" Where did he just go? He's gazing past me, pensive, wistful, maybe even a little melancholy.

"In every genre there are greats," he said quietly. "Too many to choose one."

"I guess that's true." Maybe he's thinking about how he's dedicated his life and never made that final cut. For an artist, that must be crushing. Did he play anything tonight that sounded like an original? I'm not sure and I'm not going to ask him. We may have more in common than I realized at first. Maybe his life feels like mine: one long groundhog day of covers. His mood has shifted pulling mine along with it. I intended to tap into his vulnerability but I didn't expect him to allow me in. I can see and feel his tender heart. That changes things.

"Anything else you want to know?"

"Do you feel like going deeper?" Why the hell did I say that? I meant to say I thought I had enough material to write the kind of story the paper looks for.

"Deeper?" He furrowed his brow, watching me intently.

"Yeah, I mean, we could delve . . ."

"What do you want?" he interrupted.

Good question. What do I really want now? My foot has slipped off the brake and slammed onto the gas pedal. "I want you to . . . "

"Kiss you?" he interjected, pulling me close and brushing his lips across my cheek just as I turned to face him. My mouth slightly open to speak, touched his briefly. We held still there. He pressed his body closer and kissed me with conviction. I hadn't realized how much I'd been yearning for his touch, for the feel of his arms around me and the tangy taste of tequila on his lips. "What more do you want to know?" he asked softly.

"I want to know how your guitar feels when you're playing your favorite song." I whispered. He kissed me more insistently, his tongue exploring mine. "I want to feel like that song," I sighed with shameless desire.

I felt him push aside that invisible barrier he had established between us in the beginning. I realized then that I had been leaning against it and as it fell, my energy streamed into the opening he'd created. He peered into my eyes then and I could see in his, exactly which curve we'd be careening off soon.

"You want to feel like that song?" He took the pen out of my hand and brushed the soggy napkins aside and whispered, "I feel a new favorite coming on." He kissed me, stoking my cheek in such a tender way, I nearly melted. "Let's make a new melody. Strumming some fresh chords out of you feels natural and easy. Are we done here?"

"I think I've got what I need to write a music lover's article." It was easy. And he has no idea how easy playing my song will be.

"Then let's go make some new harmonies." He slapped a big bill on the little table, shoved the pile of napkins into my jeans back pocket and pulled me out of the booth behind him. "Come with me, delicious woman."

"Oh yeah . . . I'm coming, rock star." Yup. He's perfect.

The moments of happiness we enjoy take us by surprise.
It is not that we seize them, but that they seize us.
  ~ Ashley Montagu

It's Just Lunch

"Let's have lunch, Savannah. Do you like sushi?"
    "Sushi? Sounds great, Greg. I love sushi."

Savannah and I are working on a project together. We've been having a lively phone conversation for over 40 minutes. I like her. She's beautiful, intelligent, and sexy as hell. We laugh. We flirt. I like to spend time with her whenever we can. It's possible that I think about her lips and her body a little too often and maybe a little too graphically. Why is this an issue? She only recently ended her marriage. I haven't.

We've had lunch together a couple of times before, but today on the phone, her laughter brings to mind images of her naked. Naked in bed with me. I'm overcome with the urge to have sex with her, make love to her. While she chats on about something I've lost track of at the moment, I email my favorite sushi place in the Metropolitan Hotel. I want to make some special arrangements. I want to continue our conversation sipping some sake alone with her, taking it further if she will. That's my plan anyway, and I'm excited with the prospect. I know she won't be expecting anything like that. But I also know she likes me too, even if she's never given any indication of having the same interest in me. I'm hand-on-cock-hard, drifting in lusty thoughts of pleasure with her when . . .

"Greg? Hey. Are you still there? I said where would you like me to meet you?"

"Oh. Yeah. Hey, I'll pick you up. I'm just over at my office. I can be there in about 10 minutes. How's that sound?"

"Okay, but I'm dressed casually today. I only came in to push some papers around my desk. I wasn't expecting to see anyone, so if jeans, a t-shirt and flip flops are alright, I'll see you in 10."

I wonder where we're going? I guess I can finish this stuff up tomorrow. Where's my bag? I'm sure I need a quick fix of lipstick and a hair brush. I wish I'd at least worn some shoes, and a bra. Why didn't I wear a damn bra? I hope my blue cashmere sweater is in the car. Do I have anything out there that would make me look more put together? Why does this matter so much to me right now? It's just lunch with Greg. Why am I feeling so nervous?

"Hey, jeans are fine. I'm sure you look great."

If things go well she won't have to worry about what she has on for long. I can't help grinning about that prospect until the thought of her refusing wipes it off my face. She might. What if she does? I enjoy her friendship. I don't want anything to interfere with that. But man, I really want something to come of this. I really want to make her come. I really want to . . . Jesus. Stop it!

When I pull up, she's out in the parking lot rummaging around the back seat of her car. Her adorable rump is up in the air; her low-cut jeans, stretched below the curve of her hips, show just a peek of her butt. A flip-flop dangles from the foot of the leg stretched out behind her. God, she's so natural. She doesn't act like she knows the effect she has on men. On me.

She's backing out of her car as I walk up behind her. A sweet spicy scent, like soap, drifts my way. I picture my hands grabbing her hips as she backs into me. I can feel my hands already tangled in her hair, my body pressed against hers, touching her skin, kissing her mouth, sticking my . . . Stop it! I'm totally preoccupied with thoughts of touching her breasts, her thighs, having sex with her. Man, I got to get a grip.

"Hey, what are you looking for?

"Wow, Greg, that was quick. I was just looking for something else to wear, alas in vain. There's nothing back here but my gym bag, sorry."

Of course, he looks as handsome as always, kind of rumpled and somehow sophisticated at the same time. I look like I should be weeding the garden or cleaning house rather than going out for sushi with an attractive guy.

"You look great. You don't need to change a thing. Ready to go?"

I'm ready. Ready to grab her ass right here. Restrain yourself, man.

"I guess so."

When he opens the door of his black BMW, he touches my back lightly as he guides me in. I sink into the deep leather seat and watch him slide in easily behind the wheel. I love his natural unassuming manner. I notice as I have many times, every time I've seen him, how good he looks in a rustic but distinctive way. It's as though he's given his wardrobe some thought, but only in passing. Today he's wearing dark brown cords, a pale blue denim shirt with the sleeves rolled, a tooled belt, and there's a yellow sweater thrown in the back seat. As we pull out of the parking lot he turns to me smiling, his hazel eyes twinkling. He seems excited about something.

"I'm taking you to my favorite sushi place."

"Which is your favorite?"

There's something different about him today. His energy is edgy, even a little nervous. I haven't experienced that with him before. I wonder what's up. He's usually so confident and together. It must be my imagination.

"You'll see when we get there. You'll love it."

I can't help chuckling. I'm trying to sound both mysterious and nonchalant. I glance at her to check her reaction. She's watching me intently. That's one of the things about her that's so appealing and also scary. She's always paying attention, always alert and aware.

We met when I was pitching a design concept to her firm. She's bright and savvy when it comes to business. Some of her observations have helped me implement some creative solutions to issues I've had with my current pain-in-the-ass project. Using her suggestions has greatly calmed my anxiety about it.

"And where is there?"

Why is he acting so oddly? Rather than answer, he clicks on the stereo.

"Is that the song you were telling me you loved?"

Sarah McLachlan? I wouldn't have expected him to listen to someone like her. He's a guy's guy, not exactly macho, but this sentimental? Who knew? Hmmm. And this song: 'I Will Remember You' is one of my favorites.

"Yeah. I love her music. Her songs touch me somehow. She's Canadian, did you know that? What? Guys can't dig chick music? Why are you staring at me like that?"

She is. She's laughing softly. She winked. What in hell does that mean? How do women always get the upper hand? She didn't even have to try. Glad we don't have far to go. Jesus. This isn't as easy as I thought it would be. Okay, I know she's not easy, but now she's probably thinking. When women get quiet and start thinking, a barrage of questions can come next, usually ones I don't want to answer. She's probably trying to figure me out, probably already has. I thought this would be easier. At least she's hanging with me today.

"I like her a lot too and I really love this song. I'm impressed, Greg. Her lyrics touch on such deep emotional themes."

Since when do guys enjoy anything that evokes deep feelings? He says he does. Interesting. I would never have guessed.

"Well, here we are."

When we pull up under the canopy at the entrance to the hotel, I turn to look at her. The expression of concern on her face stops me cold. I plant a smile on my face, hoping to hide both my nervousness and my ulterior motive. The valet takes my keys.

"Here for sushi," I say with false confidence. He nods and opens her door, flashing me a crooked conspiratorial grin. Why?

Does he know about my special requests? Not likely. But he's a guy, and she's gorgeous.

"This sushi bar? Greg, I am definitely not dressed for this place." *I'm a mess. Damn it!*

"Savannah, you look gorgeous no matter what you're wearing. Who cares? Let's enjoy ourselves. It's just lunch."

She's pouting. She's irresistible. I plant my arm around her shoulder casually. I can't help myself. I brush her lips lightly with mine and try to act as if it's nothing, like we're just friends, like it's something we always do. She doesn't pull away. Now I can't wipe this grin off my face.

"Very kind of you, Greg. Thanks."

He's kissing me? What if someone we know sees us here today? Thank God the lobby is nearly empty. I forget where the sushi bar is; I think we have to go up a couple floors. He has his arm around me. Is that okay? Is it okay that I like the way his arm feels around me? He's more relaxed, more cheerful now, chatting me up about how we timed lunch just right, no crowds. The elevator door opens and we step in. We're alone. He's pulling me closer. What's this about? We get out onto a floor of guest rooms. Why? He leads me a short distance down the hall to one of them. He's got a key in his hand. Opening the door, he waits for me to enter.

"After you, beautiful."

She's not moving, she's standing there frozen in place.

"Please come in, Savannah."

Did my voice just waver? The room looks perfect, just the way I ordered it. What if she won't come in? What will I do? I take her hand and pull her through the door. She lets me, she's starting to get the picture, biting her lip, glancing around the room. I lock the door behind us. She's silent. I can't help it, I kiss the back of her neck. Now she turns and looks up at me.

"What are we doing?

I can barely muster a whisper. There's a small round table set for two adorned with a single white orchid. Several covered dishes with delectable aromas, a fragrant steaming pot of jasmine tea and a large decanter of hot sake are arranged around the orchid. The bed is turned back. The shades are drawn against the midday sun. Soft music is coming from somewhere.

"What are we doing here, Greg?"

"Savannah, don't be upset. I wanted to surprise you. I was hoping you'd be pleased. You've probably guessed the reason for all this by now. I just want to hold you. I've wanted to hold you and kiss you since we met. I guess I thought if I surprised you with something special you'd understand how I feel about you. I guess I hoped you wouldn't resist. I wanted you to relax and enjoy yourself. I want to make love with you, Savannah. Let me make love to you."

Damn, I'm spilling my guts all over the place. I'm not good at this. She's wearing an expression of what? Not horror, not fear, but obviously she's completely surprised. Does that mean she's never thought about something like this, with me? Crap. It's all I can think about.

"So this is why you're acting so mysteriously."

Maybe it's true that I enjoy spending time with him, talking with him, flirting with him. I guess if I'm honest, I'd admit I've thought about kissing those yummy lips, but having sex with him? I've never considered that prospect. He's married. I haven't even thought about dating again since my divorce was final. I feel shaky. No wonder I've felt so nervous since he asked me to lunch. I must have been having some kind of precognition. Why didn't I pick up on his intentions before we got this far?

"Please. I've been aching to hold you. Just let me hold you. I can be happy with that, but I want to make love to you, didn't you know that?"

Now I've become a pathetic beggar but at least she isn't trying to leave. Maybe I'm imagining it, wishing it, she looks like she needs some support. If I hold her close, hold her steady, maybe she won't be so tense, maybe she'll trust me. I swear I can feel her melting into my arms. She's looking up at me confused, uncertain, thinking. Oh God, Savannah, don't think. Even if she's feeling conflicted she's not resisting me, she's holding me too.

"Savannah. Ahhh, at last. If you only knew."

He's holding me in his arms, and I'm not only letting him, I need him to hold me. I feel dizzy, faint, knocked off balance by this unexpected turn of events. What's most surprising to me right now is not that I am here with him, that's strange enough. It's that I want to be here with him. How long has that feeling been hidden from me? I don't know what to do. What am I doing?

She's not pulling away. She's softening, letting me touch her. She's warming up to me. Her body so close to mine is driving me insane. I gotta slow down, slow way down. Kiss her while I can. I'm an idiot.

He's kissing me. Tentative, waiting for me to respond. I can feel him, his passion, his need. He wants me. Oh God! Why am I reaching up to him? Why are my arms around his neck? These feelings, these almost forgotten sensations,. What am I doing? His lips are luscious. Luscious. I want this. He's slipping his hands under my shirt. He's touching me, he's touching my breasts. Oh God! I'm not stopping him. I should be resisting him. I can't resist.

No bra? No surprise. It's impossible not to notice how her round tits bounce along when she walks. It's impossible not to notice how these perfect handfuls of sweet flesh make my dick hard the minute I see them. Her soft nipples should be in my mouth. It's warm in here but she's shivering. She's letting me unzip her jeans, she's not stopping me. No panties? Fuck! Her skin is like silk. My hands on the curve of her hips, her ass. Fuck!

"Jesus, Savannah, you feel so good."

Thank you. And thank you, God. I want her. I wanted to seduce her. I only hoped she would be receptive. But, goddamn, no panties, no bra? Her skin, her tits, her spicy scent, her hair. Damn. She's hooked me with no effort..

His hands, his touch, his breath on my neck, his lips sliding down my throat. I feel like I'm in a dream. He's touching me and I feel layers of pent-up passion beginning to release. I've been so busy for so long I didn't even realize I still possessed these feelings. I didn't know I possessed this need about to explode from my body.

"Greg . . ."

Did my voice make any sound? I'm not sure. He just slipped my shirt over my head and dropped it on the floor. I'm opening his shirt. I want to lay my cheek on his smooth chest. What the hell am I doing? I need to pull away from him, just a little. I've got to get my bearings, catch my breath. God! He's gorgeous.

"Savannah . . ."

Now I'm whispering. Breathe. Slow down man, don't spook her. Pour some sake.

He's offering me hot sake in a tiny black porcelain cup. I shouldn't take it but I do. We sip silently staring into each other's eyes. I'm making a valiant and so far unsuccessful effort not to think about the consequences of where we are and what we're doing. If we stop right now there will be nothing to feel guilty about, nothing to justify. Well, almost nothing. But that isn't going to happen. I don't want that to happen. I don't want to stop now.

"Savannah, do you have any idea what this means to me?"

No, she doesn't. It's clear she doesn't know how she is, how she makes me feel. My heart is pounding standing next to her like this looking into her beach glass colored eyes, softer now, almost shy. Her sunny blonde hair is always just slightly mussed up, like it's windblown. She makes me feel alive and free, like a day of sailing in a good wind. Her lips, those pouty lips, always look so ready to be kissed. I need to kiss her. She's driving me crazy. I wasn't expecting to feel like this, so emotional. What am I going to do now?

"More please."

I drain my cup. I need more liquid courage. He kisses my breast with his sake-warmed lips. Warm sake kisses heating up my juices. I hand him my empty cup and fumble with his belt. He stops statue-still mid-pour, then refills my cup. I take another long sip. It's so good. My nerves and tense muscles begin to relax.

I pour us each another cup. Sake. She likes it. I like that. She sips hers slowly now before finally handing her empty cup back to me. She's warming up. I'm on fire. Is she ready? Slow down, slow down. Get a hold of yourself.

I open his belt, unzip his cords and pull them down. I can't believe I'm doing this. I want to. I'm curious, inflamed, seeing his body, feeling him through his faded blue striped boxers, I can't breathe. I slip my hands under the elastic, sliding his skivvies down to his knees. Oh my God! Freed from constraint, he's beautiful, impressive, hard. The shape and length of him triggers an aggressive desire I didn't know was in me. I touch him. His hungry greedy kisses. Oh God!

She's got a grip on me. I've gotta hold on. I back her up to the bed. Her lips, her mouth, hungry like mine. She's consuming me. She means it. I slide my hand between her thighs and feel her wet secret place. She's wet. Can't fake that. She's ready. She wants it. She wants me. Jesus. God.

He's laying me down at the foot of the bed and spreading my legs. Standing between them, hovering over me, his beautiful hard cock is just inches from my mouth. Oh God! Where am I? What am I doing? I want to put my mouth around him. I reach for him and pull him toward me. I take him into my mouth. He moans. It pleases him. I can taste him, that first sweet drop. I want more. He's gripping my thighs. I can't stop now.

"Savannah. Christ."

I have to pull away from her. I have to stop her. I don't want to. I have to. Look at her. Her beautiful mouth on me like that. I have to pull away. I'm going to come. I know I can't hold on much longer like this. I want to experience her fully, completely. I pull away.

"You first. I want to taste you too, I want to come inside of you. You're driving me crazy."

I lift her body, light as air, onto the middle of the bed. I want to touch her, lick her, kiss her everywhere. I need to taste her. I need to please her. I need . . . I need to hold on. I want to please her. I want to get inside her.

He lowers himself over me, kissing first my lips then my breasts. My pulse quickens, my heart is racing. He gently spreads my thighs and runs his hands slowly up the insides of them until he comes to my opening. I feel myself begin to tense. He leans into me then and with the tip of his tongue, he tastes my bud. My body lurches toward him involuntarily. Now the length of his tongue explores my every part. The soft swelling sides of my clitoris, my slippery smooth opening, my labia. He's pleasuring me, every inch of me. His tongue dips into my vagina and swirls like he's stirring a cocktail. It makes me giggle, I can't help it. Intentionally, expertly, he rolls his tongue over the top of my clit, circling it in the same way. Light licks, gentle sucks, nervous tension evaporating from my body. Sounds coming from me I haven't heard in years. His warm mouth devouring me.

His fingers slip inside of me. He finds my spot, works it with precision, coaxes from me a jolt, a rumbling explosion. I'm coming. From deep inside myself a volcanic orgasm erupts, the surprising intensity of it an earth-moving ecstasy. I scream. Did I just scream? Oh God, oh God!

Her fingers are tangled in my hair, holding my head in place. She wants it, she wants me. She's coming. The creamy sweet taste of her exploding in my mouth. She moans. I moan. I suck her clit, work her spot. Her nipples harden again. She writhes, she quakes, she's letting herself go with it. Look at her, look at her like that. Jesus God. Grab her hips, pull her up, I gotta get inside of her. I'm in. Plunging. In. Fuck, Savannah! Fuck me.

Oh! I feel my juices erupt like a geyser. He lifts me, holding my hips up sinking in deep. I take a deep breath. We make contact. I gasp. He stops, throws his head back, closes his eyes. My orgasm subsides just enough to be conscious of every sensation.

The smooth cool muscles on his arms, my fingers tangled in those silvery curls falling over his ears and forehead, his open mouth still wet with my cum.

Now there's a new sensation, the intense pulsation of his cock deep inside of me. Pressure is building like in the eye of a hurricane. First a momentary calm, a stillness, before he tightens his grip on my hips and starts to move. The storm is moving, slowly gathering strength, power and momentum. He thrusts deep inside of me, then deeper still. He fucks me with all he's got. He's a raging storm, a primal force. I can feel him pry open my sexual core.

As I'm riding her, she molds herself to me. I feel her building to the next level. I feel her nails digging into my ass. I hear her call out my name as she jolts forward. I pump her hard. We explode together. We ignite. We're spontaneous combustion. My hot spurt shoots long and deep inside of her. I'm obliterated.

He collapses on top of me, his entire body shaking, his cock throbbing inside of me. I feel our cells thrumming. I can hear them. I'm so overcome with emotion, I can't move, I can't breathe. He rolls off of me onto his back, lying next to me. His eyes are closed, mine are filling with tears. I curl up beside him, clutching him, unable to stop thrumming. So much feeling, such intense sensation. Finally our breathing calms, returning to here. Is he asleep? No. He turns to me, studying me, looking deeply into my eyes.

"I knew it. I knew we would be great together, I could feel it, I've dreamed about it, now I know for sure."

She kisses my cheek, she fits folded into my side, and she's silent. She's quiet now. She's never quiet.

"I know you're thinking. I know what you're thinking. Please stop thinking."

I want what we just had to be separate from everything and everyone else in our lives. I want her to enjoy this moment. I just wanted her to enjoy this moment with me.

"Please, Savannah. Look, we're good. This is good. It's just lunch."

I look at him more closely now. He's serious. A smile sneaks up and spreads across my face. A cavalcade of mirth rises up from my belly. I have to laugh. I begin to laugh hard. I can't stop. He catches my wave and laughs too. Where and how we're just having lunch is so funny, and too complicated to think about at this moment. Wrapped in each other's arms, we laugh until tears run down our cheeks, until our bellies ache. This luscious moment of bliss and laughter is the best lunch I've ever had. It's heaven. I have no doubt I'll be doing nothing but thinking about all this later, but not now. Did he really know it would be like this?

"Whatever made you imagine that I would agree to this to-day? And even more mysteriously, how did you know how to please me so, well, so completely?"

I please her. She's pleased. How did I know? I don't have to think that over.

"I knew the minute we met. You have a kind of fuck-me way about you."

Crap! What did I just say? I didn't mean to say it that way.

"What? What do you mean? What did I do? What did I say? I'm positive I wasn't thinking anything like that when we first met, or ever!"

"I know. I'm sure you weren't. It isn't anything you do or say; it's something intangible, sensual."

Damn it! "You're not overtly sexual, but you do have sexuality streaming from you." That didn't help. "It precedes you and follows you." I keep making it worse, damn.

"It's hard to explain and it's hard to be anywhere near you and not be hard." I laughed, she didn't. "I've watched the way other guys react and sometimes try not to react to you. I guess it's just your way, your energy."

Crap. What have I done? She's pulling away, pulling the sheet over her delicious body. How the hell am I going to defuse this? The last fucking thing in the fucking world I want right now is anything getting in the way of being with her, her being upset, her withdrawing from me. I'm a fucking idiot.

How should I to respond to this? He's waiting for my reaction. I see the pained expression on his face, feel the tension in his body. I feel it in mine. He thinks I'm upset and I probably should be, but the fact is I've been told things like this before, a number of times. My ex-husband, Frank, still tells me this. It's probably meant to be flattering but it's more disconcerting. I guess the implication is that I am desirable and sexy without effort. That should be a good thing, shouldn't it? It's not. In my experience it doesn't draw men toward me, quite the contrary. I know men, including Frank, are attracted to me, but it's mostly because they're thinking about fucking me, otherwise it seems they'd rather avoid me. I want to drop this now. I don't want to think about it and have it ruin this moment with Greg. I can see that he wishes he never brought it up. That's endearing.

"I'm starving . . . sushi?"

Thank you, God! "Me too. Sushi. Let's try these maguro first." She's decided to let this slide. I'm saved. She's smiling. Her face is soft. She's not angry. She forgives me, I can feel it. God, she's beautiful. Beautiful inside too.

"Here. Let's finish this sake while it's still warm."

I can't take my eyes off of her mouth. The way her lips touch the cup. I take it from her. I want to kiss her warm sake lips. I have to. She drops the chopsticks she's fiddling with and leans closer to me, her nipples grazing my arm. She kisses me back, then pulls away again. She picks up a maguro with her fingers. Licking her bottom lip, she slowly fills her mouth. She's watching me. Her eyes are so seductive, so damn sexy delicious. She's playing with me.

She lifts another one from the plate and feeds it to me the same way. Her tongue slides over her bottom lip. Her mouth is open. I picture how it looked, how it felt wrapped around my cock. Hell, she's making me hard again already. She's so damn fuckable. I knew she would be, she can't help it, she can't hide it. I want her again. Now.

"Savannah, please say we can have lunch again soon."

Her green eyes sparkle as she winks at me, licks her fingers and takes a last sip of sake. Now she's laughing softly. She moves closer and kisses me. Climbs on top of me, shoving me back on the bed. She's straddling me, making my dick rock solid. I'm guessing this means Yes!

"Does this mean yes, beautiful woman?"

I don't have to think about that answer. How could I say no? He's hard again and so yummy, I want him now.

"This means Yes. It's just lunch isn't it?"

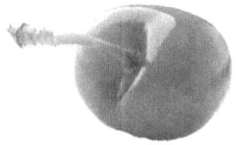

*". . . when something happens and you notice what it is . . .
check your watch in seconds . . ."*
  ~ The I Ching Moderne

Professor William

M any years ago, when I discovered the I Ching, that ancient
Chinese oracle known as the book of changes, I practiced
using it as a guide to discern what was happening in the moment
and which direction to take. As time went on, often over drinks
with friends, I extracted and recorded snippets from our ani-
mated conversations and developed a second-by-second, *I Ching
Moderne*, for my own amusement. A page for each second in a
minute, those sixty pages eventually became filled with obscure
comments. They may not provide the sage wisdom of the ancient one, but it's uncanny how in any given second, the *Moderne*
comments can offer me a profoundly contextual match in meaning for a particular point in time.

  6:16 p.m.
  *". . . it's only because we're who we are . . . that we would be in
a place like this . . . "*

  William is a professor at the University of Washington. William loves baseball. William, whom I discovered is an avid Yankees fan, was enthusiastically drinking his way through tonight's
World Series game at this popular neighborhood pub. Tall and
sophisticated, a bit gangly, six foot six I'd guess, blond, blue-eyed,
kind of Nordic-looking, William was a little drunk.

  He was occupying a strategically-positioned stool below the
TV screen. I stood pressed against him, trying to squeeze in at
this crowded bar. We were both vying for the bartender's attention. I think it was because I managed to attract the barkeep's eye
so quickly that William invited me to join him for a cocktail.

A few moments ago, my girlfriend deserted me for a swarthy-looking fellow, who had captured her attention at the end of the bar. I accepted William's invitation. Glancing down the bar again, I didn't see either of them. She and I had been uptown for a couple drinks and some appetizers before deciding to drop into this place. She insisted we check it out, having heard it was always teeming with men. It certainly was tonight for obvious reasons. I strained to get a view of the rest of the pub, but I didn't see her anywhere. I wasn't concerned.

"I've claimed this seat right here for its bird's-eye view of the game. Join me? We'll share it," William suggested. "But before we begin, and not that it matters in the long run mind you, I'd like to know who you're cheering for tonight." This he asked me all in the same breath as, "Hello, would you like a drink, and let's sit here at the bar so we can best see the screen."

"Who's playing?" I asked demurely. Of course I knew who was playing, but I couldn't care less who won.

"Good Lord!" His hands, with such long delicate fingers he might have been a concert pianist, covered his eyes as he moaned and shook his head.

"Not that it matters in the long run," I teased, "or even this very moment, but I'd bet on the Yankees to win. I could just as easily settle for the Dodgers. Secretly, I like the name of the Cardinals best." He chuckled as he peeked through his fingers, and I noticed that he had one eyebrow raised as he stared at me. He finished his drink as the allure of the TV screen distracted him for a moment. I motioned to the bartender and called out, "I'll have what he's having."

6:33 p.m.

"*. . . nothing matters that much . . . oh yes it does . . . no it really doesn't . . .* "

"Well, you're a quite a tease, aren't you?" He smiled, turning his stool toward me, shifting his attention from the game to my face. "Hmmm, and alarmingly attractive as well, a winning and potentially lethal combination."

My evening had been on the verge of becoming a cliché for hours already. I've collected thousands of them for entertainment. There seemed to be no good reason not to indulge myself.

"How 'bout them Yankees?" I quipped cheerfully.

During the World Series, it's indefensible not to care about the outcome. I don't give a damn about baseball or any sporting events, but I thoroughly grasp the treason behind not acting as if I am avid about The Series. It's practically un-American. Especially so in a sports pub with swilling males. Unless I was planning to buy my own drinks tonight, I would have to carry on some kind of knowledgeable baseball conversation. I could. In the car, on the way over, I had turned the dial to the sports radio station broadcasting the Series. I learned that it was game three between the Yankees, who had won the first two in New York, and the Dodgers, who now had the home field advantage. Those were enough stats for me to sound as though I were in the know and cared.

He fairly squealed with delight. You'd think I'd just hit one out of the park. "Oh! You're not only adorable but a good sport. What's more, you're astute enough to lean toward the right dugout!" He called down the bar and ordered two more drinks. "Let's get this game started, shall we?"

"Okay, let's. Come here often? What's your sign? What do you do?" I asked as he stared at my breasts seemingly confused by the three standard pub questions in quick succession. I doubted he was aware that our game had already begun and I got the feeling I might be slinging clichés all night for my amusement alone.

"What? Oh . . . let's see . . . uh yes. I do come here often, and yes, I not only live in this area, I work near here as well. I am a professor of marine biology and fisheries. I do research here at the university. I'm a Scorpio and your breasts have captivated me. Your turn." He stood up and again waved two slender fingers at the bartender, glanced at the screen, then leaned closer to me and almost whispered, "My name is William, no one has ever called me Will or Willy, probably because I never became a ball player."

6:53 p.m.

". . . this line is for you . . . help yourself . . . no silly, it's not cocaine . . . it's just a line . . ."

"All's fair in love and war, William Willy Will. What's your poison? What's your pleasure?" I might have told him that I was not from around here nor do I work near here, but I didn't feel like divulging such impersonal information. "I'm not so sure about your breasts at this point, but I can tell you that I am an Aries and my name is Savannah." It was already clear to me that I was well on my way to some inappropriate behavior tonight.

I stood up and waved two fingers at the bartender and sat back down. At that moment, the Dodgers hit a double and the pub erupted in pandemonium. William pounded the sticky bar with his fists, rattling drinks all the way down. No one seemed to notice but me as the place was in an uproar of evenly divided cheers and jeers. "Go Cardinals!" I screamed at the top of my lungs, turning a number of confused heads in my direction including an incredulous William, before he burst into loud peals of laughter.

The Yankees were still in the lead and maybe he felt confident they would keep it, or maybe he was intoxicated enough to forget about the game for a minute, or maybe he was captivated by more than my breasts. He reached for me and wrapping me in his long arms, pulled me close and kissed me so suddenly it surprised us both. He let me go in the next moment and took a long sip of his drink.

"Forgive me. I don't know what got into me." He finished his drink and reached for the next one waiting in line. So did I.

"I must say, you're very funny, Savannah. Still, I can't help taking your lips quite seriously. I fear I may need to beg your forgiveness in advance as I am overcome with the most intense desire to research them more thoroughly"

"One thing leads to another. Forgive and forget. Love makes the world go round." I blurted, wondering if I could stop this Tourette's of clichés if I really needed to for any good reason. Now unleashed, it might take some effort and several more drinks, to rein them in.

William stared at me in confusion, but then his eyes drifted down to my breasts again. Pulling me even closer than before, his long arms wrapped all the way around me, crossing in the back so that those tapered fingers cupped the sides of my startled breasts. I put my arms around his neck and we held each other's gaze while he discreetly fondled me between innings. I reached for my glass and was taking a sip, when I noticed a slight movement between his legs. I looked down and stared at his growing bulge and so did he. A slow smile spread across his face and I found myself licking my lips. We laughed and he licked my lips a couple times before kissing them again hungrily.

"That's the way the ball bounces. Time is of the essence. Live like there's no tomorrow." I spewed when we came up for air.

7:12 p.m.

". . . if you think this is it . . . you might be right . . . then again . . . what do you know? . . ."

William and I were on the verge of sliding into first when my girlfriend reappeared, her hair mussed and lipstick smeared. She told me she was about to take off with swarthy George, when she remembered that she had driven us tonight. Could I please drive her car to my place and she would make it up to me when she picked it up tomorrow? Before I could articulate an answer, she tossed me the keys and George pulled her back out the door. She waved gaily, blowing me a kiss. William and I both watched transfixed as the door slowly closed behind them. Another couple pushed in, hooting greetings to friends across the room and broke our spell.

"We might consider indulging in an interlude of our own between innings." William suggested, nibbling on my ear. "My van is parked just outside. We could adjourn momentarily to contemplate the meaning of all this. The Yanks are ahead and I am certain they will hold their lead. Why don't we listen to the game out there while you assist me with some important research concerning your lips? Quite possibly a more in-depth investigation of your breasts could be in order, as well."

"Professor William, are you saying it just so happens that you have a van handy, one that you have converted into a mobile research laboratory? And, are you saying that your interests and expertise extend beyond baseball and marine life?" I sighed in relief at producing two relatively coherent questions.

The professor's ice blue eyes twinkled mischievously as he tucked a strand of my hair behind my ear, evaluating me beyond my mammary assets. "Well now, you're quite a catch aren't you, Savannah? Definitely not the usual fish out of water type found flopping around this bar. I believe you're a keeper."

He stood up, handed me another glass, grabbing one for himself from our line-up. Knocking it back, he encouraged me to do the same.

7:39 p.m.

"*. . . pink elephants . . . standing in the middle of the living room . . . don't always understand why they are there . . . much less why they're being ignored . . .*"

For some odd reason, along with my cache of clichés, the I Ching Moderne was lodged in my frontal lobe this evening. There didn't seem to be anything I could do about it and there didn't seem to be much obvious relevance to marine biology, baseball or the professor, but that is never the important part of a story to me. Relevance can be made of anything and often the more incongruent the merrier.

"Catch as catch can. Carry the one. Curiosity killed the cat. How do you truly feel about diving into primordial depths, William?" I wondered out loud if he were descended from Norwegian fisher-folk.

"Fisher-folk? Oh God, no. Marine biology may be my esteemed degree and fisheries may be the sub-department that the university has deemed to assign me, but it is my minor degree in anthropology that is major to me. My fascination and private field of research is the intersection of human evolution and vanishing marine species. However, baseball and especially The Series, particularly when the Yankees are playing, take precedence over any of that. And now, since you've appeared, I have developed an engorged interest in lips and breasts that I think ought to be taken more seriously. Only if you agree, of course." He paused, exchanging our empty glasses for the last in our stockpile, then once again waved two experienced fingers at the bartender. "Dipping into primordial depths requires some degree of courage, wouldn't you say? Perhaps you have expertise in the exploration of moist and uncharted territories. Whatever the case, Savannah, I'm hooked."

"Nothing ventured, nothing gained. Man the lifeboats. Thar she blows!" I sputtered, forced to acknowledge that under the influence of alcohol my mind takes on the qualities of a gill net. Clichés were swimming through like krill.

He laughed heartily, picked up the two fresh drinks in one hand, slipped them deftly into the pocket of his linen jacket and signed the tab. The glasses held securely in place with one hand, he draped his other arm around my shoulders dwarfing me as we left the pub and sauntered down the street to his van.

"Why, even in heels, you're no bigger than a minnow, and you couldn't be any prettier, with those sea green eyes and corn silk hair. How did I manage to be so fortunate this evening?" He held me tightly as we strolled down to the next block. Pointing to his vehicle with a grin, he announced affectionately, "Here she is."

I laughed out loud when I saw it. His mobile lab was an old Chevy van with a peace symbol hanging from the mirror and faded window decals of mandalas and slogans from a bygone era. Inside there was the stale lingering scent of patchouli and weed, fringed tie-dye curtains, a futon rolled up against the side, a tiny camp stove and cooler, hiking gear, fishing poles, tennis rackets, with papers and books strewn all about. William's carefully cut and moussed hair, his open shirt, sophisticated linen slacks and jacket, and expensive loafers with no socks, all made this scene even more incongruent and off balance. I was enjoying that. I slipped off my heels and threw them into the back, hiked up my skirt and climbed in. We settled into the two front seats and he turned on the game.

8:14 p.m.
". . . there's no time like the present . . . open the damn present . . ."

The old radio crackled a new score pushing the Dodgers ahead, which unleashed a torrent of expletives from William.

"What the fuck just happened? We turn our attention elsewhere for half a second and all hell breaks loose. This is intolerable."

He produced the two almost full glasses from his sloshed pocket and handed me one. Swallowing his all at once, he tossed the empty glass out the window where it shattered in the street. I sat quietly, observing this intoxicated Scandinavian work himself into a lather over a stupid game, wondering how long it would be before a holstered gendarme tapped on his window.

"Litter and it will hurt. Haste makes waste. Take no prisoners." I really wanted to say something pithy and important, but I was dizzy and had lost count of all the . . . I think they were vodka sodas . . . we had consumed. "William, I believe you have just called undue attention to this roving laboratory. I hope you don't have any ancient contraband on board that we could get busted for, or maybe I hope you do. I feel a little woozy, William. Your name is William, isn't it? I seem to have forgotten exactly why I'm sitting with you in this merry-prankster mobile."

"Hmmm, why are we sitting in this van? First, I must say that this van is indeed an experienced prankster and I harbor a great deal of fondness for it. But why we are listening to this shitty game on an old radio doesn't make any sense at all. Secondly, I am absolutely certain that my name is William, since that is all I've ever been called, as I believe I have mentioned. Thirdly, now that you have jarred me with arresting thoughts of contraband I am wondering where I hid those joints, because fourthly, your beautiful full lips and luscious breasts pressing through this soft sweater have rekindled my memory and I believe we are here to conduct some important research."

The marine biologist, fixated on mammary glands, crawled into the back of the van. He unrolled the futon, closed all the curtains, dug out an old candle in a jar, and produced a single joint which he lit and passed to me before scrunching a sleeping bag into a pillow and reclining on the futon. I took one hit and realized immediately that it was not in my best interest to become more disoriented than I already was, and handed it back. He apparently felt the same because he stubbed it out and returned it to the tin it came from.

"Won't you join me back here in my research lab? It's a quantum leap in comfort over these front seats, and that includes those crappy bar stools as well." He sat up and reached for my hand to assist me over the console.

"Heaven forbid. Jumping Jehoshaphat. Great balls of fire." I was far more inebriated than I realized as I stumbled, then got tangled up in my skirt, tripped over his legs and landed square on top of him with a thud. "A thousand pardons. A million thanks." I mumbled, laying my head on his chest, trying to gather my swirling wits about me.

"This is an excellent starting point for the preliminary investigative work I had in mind," he mused, enthusiastically embracing one breast and one butt cheek.

"A rolling stone gathers no moss. The early bird catches the worm. All's well that ends well." I kissed him, or tried to, missing his lips completely, instead landing a wet one on his chin before my lips slipped off and onto his neck. He tasted salty and smelled faintly of soap. I liked it. I made a second successful attempt, continuing with a foray into his open and willing mouth with my tongue.

William's hands slid under my skirt and brushed over my rear appreciatively. Appraising the outline of my silken panties as I sat astraddle him, he pulled me forward to kiss his lips again. My hair, spilling out of its tie-back, covered his face.

"Savannah, your fragrant blonde waves are inducing delirium, I may lose control at any moment." He murmured, slipping those hands with the long slender fingers up under my loose sweater. Underneath, I was wearing only a camisole and his fingers easily found their way to my nipples. He softly pinched and rolled them, testing for firmness, and as he did, I squirmed and wiggled noticing that he was also firming up nicely directly beneath my dampening crotch.

"Oh!" I gasped between breathless kisses that had started to wander beyond the perimeters of our mouths.

"Oh indeed!" he muttered, rolling over and toppling me from my perch.

8:59 p.m.

". . . it's all in the timing . . . anything at all is possible when timed properly . . ."

The Series announcers prattled on through an uneventful inning, scarcely noticed by either of us. Now on top of me, William continued his inquiry of my breasts with his lips and tongue as I stared at the faded tie-dye curtains in fascination. The lights of passing cars shone through making them appear to move like kaleidoscopes. Although I was enjoying myself, I wasn't overly vested in the research at this point. I knew I was drunk and so was he. I was easily distracted until he yanked down my panties and I felt his long slender fingers gathering moist evidence of life in the deep cavern between my thighs.

"A world of wonder exists in here," he began to explain in a scholarly manner. "I can assume by my palpations, that an arousal system has been activated, as evidenced by the presence of a certain viscous fluid I have detected. Please take note of that if you will, I believe it is of some significance to our research data. I wonder what kind of kinesthetic or chemical reaction might occur if I were to add saliva to this incubating liquid that appears to be the emanating from your primordial depth."

His tongue, at the moment, was measuring the distance from my lips to my neck to my breast, and had become momentarily distracted by a nipple. Methodically and thoroughly examining them both, he pulled first one into his mouth to savor and suckle, before sampling the other, smacking his lips in satisfaction. His calculating fingers continued to explore the slippery primordial parameters of my world of wonder, which was happily responding in waves of pulsating pleasure, contracting around his probing fingers.

Now I was feeling everything with focused intensity. Although my mind was oddly dissociated, my body enthusiastically submitted to the lab work being conducted by the fascinated professor. Changing position, he sat back on his haunches, his head colliding with the low ceiling of his roving science lab and studiously peeled off my panties and skirt, tossing them aside. As he spread my legs wide, his curious mouth roamed the length and width of my quivering slit. My jaw and fists involuntarily clenched as his tongue and lips nibbled on my bait. My nipples hardened and my body convulsed again in splendor. Behind my closed eyes all the brilliant colors, shapes and angles of a kaleidoscope danced and sparkled like an acid flashback. My body vibrated deliciously, and in my mind's inner eye I saw myself illuminated radiantly from the inside out.

"Oh my God! Look at you," he gasped hoarsely, unbuckling his belt, unzipping his pants and pulling them off so quickly I was still coming when he plunged deeply into me, rocking me with his thrusting. I clutched him tightly to me as he exploded passionately and violently inside of me. "Holy galactic!" he shouted. "We're going super-nova."

9:27 p.m.

". . . and then there was that time when you blew my . . . you know . . . oh never mind . . ."

We lay there in shock, the impact from the combustion of our chemical reaction rendering us unable to move. We'd apparently blown up the roving lab, I couldn't see anything but swirling kaleidoscope colors. I continued to vibrate, my womb filled with him and his sticky juice until he withered enough to slip out, the remainder of his essence spilling onto the futon for posterity. He laid his head between my breasts and sighed deeply.

"Lord have mercy," he whispered. "What a fool I've been. I thought I knew something of the ways of research, but I completely forgot that truths emerge spontaneously and leaps of evolution can occur in the most unexpected ways."

The radio announcers were excitedly recapping the game, which as we became more present, forced us to realize it was over and we hadn't even noticed. "Who did they say won?" he mumbled, bending his ear toward the front to discern what they were babbling about, but making no effort to move from where he was.

"A thing worth doing is worth doing well. Time marches on. Everything has its season." I murmured. "I believe they said the Cardinals won."

"Oh good Lord! You crazy sexy girl." He laughed as he pulled himself up onto his elbow to gaze at me. "Do you comprehend the monumental significance to me of not giving a rip about the outcome of this game? Coming so deeply inside of you, witnessing you glow like phosphorous on a moonlit sea, feeling you even now continuing to quiver in your own strange and seductive rhythms, has diverted my passionate attention from baseball to your slippery mysterious depths. Right now, even your drunken clichés are more meaningful to me than all the dry science text in existence." He smoothed my hair away from my sticky neck and kissed me tenderly. "And as I am sure you are aware, the scientific method requires that research experiments be repeatable. That means we will be required to replicate these procedures enough times to satisfy those demands and verify our outcomes. Only with your compliance, of course."

10:07 p.m.

". . . do you believe in God? . . . yes of course, we're very close . . . why She called me yesterday just to chat . . ."

"Easy come, easy go. Easy does it. Easy like Sunday morning." I was thinking that I would be thrilled and more than willing to dedicate my delectable experiences in the primordial depths to research, especially since the scientific model would require a series of measurable and repeatable experiments with Professor William. "You can count on me and you can type up the notes, Willy."

"The best science requires a team, Savannah. You have not only provided a worthy and intriguing hypothesis, you are also the lab specimen as well as an able research assistant. I am honored to be a part of this process and intend to devote myself to it, for the sake of science, of course." He continued to elaborate, mostly to himself, the various erotic ways he planned to conduct future research with me.

As he mused, I felt myself drifting into sleep. I vaguely realized I was not in my own bed and was dimly aware that, while he chattered, William had gotten up, turned off the radio, blown out the candle and was now pulling a sleeping bag over us. He wrapped himself around me, kissed my forehead and within seconds was snoring peacefully. The last image I remember is the colorful grin on his face as a passing car's light streamed through the tie-dye. I joined him there.

10:32 p.m.

". . . what's the very best thing? in this very moment? yes. you . . . you are the very best thing . . . oh excellent! . . ."

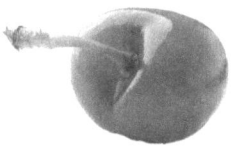

"Love is the answer.
But while you are waiting for the answer
sex raises some pretty good questions."
  ~ Woody Allen

The Drive-By

Exactly how do you describe love? I say I love him because I don't know how else to explain the tangle of emotions and feelings he evokes in me. When pressed, he'll say he loves me, too. When threatened with the extinction of what we've got going on, he'll counter with, "Baby, don't you know I love you?" In vulnerable orgasmic moments, he'll admit that he's crazy about me. The truth is that he loves fucking me.

I'm using the more desirable word love to replace the unflattering but probably more accurate term: obsession. We've fallen madly and passionately into a physical obsession. We crave it. I have no power to resist him. He's not capable of going more than a couple of days without having sex with me. My friends tell me we have a serious case of overachieving lust. What we have may not be love in the way most people would define it. But the love we make defies a typical definition. I simply cannot explain our situation adequately to myself or anyone else.

We have an intense magnetic attraction. We have colliding pheromones. We have sex that leaves us both trembling in ecstasy. We've had sex that spun us into orbit and back again laughing all the way. We've climaxed in each other's arms weeping. We've had sex that made us crazy. I have come so long and hard and continually with this man, that I can't imagine anything or anyone being better. And I can't imagine giving that up. But would I? If I met someone who offered me a more committed traditional version of love? People always ask me that question.

Aren't women supposed to want that happily-ever-after story-book fantasy? He and I don't seem to be heading there. We don't talk about it. I don't think about it. At least I try not to. What he is willing to talk about is how happy he feels when he's with me. How he knows that when I touch him, I feel him. He tells me how my eyes pierce his soul and see him. That he loves the way I smell so sweaty and sweet after having sex. The way I make him laugh. He tells me I'm beautiful. He says there's something different about me. That he can't stay away from me. But he hasn't told me he loves me.

When he first kissed me, it was so unexpectedly delicious, I was captured in that moment. His lips are full, possibly the most sensuous lips I've ever had the pleasure to experience. Just thinking about his lips on mine and where they love to roam from there, makes me shivery and damp. And he makes no bones of his need for me. His jones is immediately physical and obvious.

When he calls me with that lusty low tone of voice, when he says he's on his way, when he whispers what he wants to do with me, to me, I can come just thinking about it. I'm wet and ready when he gets here. He's tall and beautiful and muscular and there's something different about him too. It's not just that he's drop dead gorgeous. It's more than his musky scent or the contrast of his dark smooth skin. Maybe it's his strength and determination. And it's definitely his potent sexuality. It's all these things and together they kindle my body with electricity. We turn on. We both have to admit that what we do best, what we really do right is fuck.

I wasn't expecting him today. We both enjoy having our own homes and haven't made the time or space in our lives to stay with each other every night. This beautiful sunny morning, with no looming deadlines, I decided to skip work and tend to my front garden. The pleasure of puttering, watering, cutting flowers, being alone and quiet is an enjoyment I'd been yearning for. He told me, when he left early this morning, that he would be stuck in a meeting all day and was going to a Mariners game with his crew tonight. But he called from his car saying the conference ended early. He has that tone of voice. He said he's on his way. I had other plans for the afternoon. I promptly canceled them. I've rearranged my life around this man more times than I'd like to admit. I don't care. When he calls me like this, nothing else is as compelling. Nothing is more important. Thinking that I have time to freshen up before he arrives, I linger in the warmth of the sunshine. But he pulls up within minutes and parks in the drive.

"Hey baby." He calls to me from his car. "I was headed to the gym when I drove by and saw you standing out here in your garden." He pulls me into his arms. "It made me happy to know I'd secretly seen you, all sunny and busy out here." He runs his hands down my back to my cheeks. "You looked so relaxed and peaceful. I blew you a kiss. Did you catch it?" He lifts me off the ground to kiss me then sets me back down, stepping back to look me over. "I was just walking into the gym, when I flashed on the image of you bending over your flowers." His entire being is reflected in his radiant smile. "That's all it takes, baby." He pulls the bodice of my blouse out an inch and leans in for a view. "A little peek of what you got is enough to change my mind about what I want to do next." I shiver.

"Are you saying that all it takes to get you to turn around is a little peek of skin?"

"Yeah, that's all it takes, baby. And you know it. I get hard just thinking about you."

I can't help noticing the truth in that statement. Mmmmm.

"So I decided right then that a different workout was in order today." He takes the basket and shears from my hand. "Let's go in." His grin is contagious. I behold that grin and my body responds. And when I see him hung and ready like this, my depths tremble and clench. Nothing feels more important than reveling in it, experiencing him. Taking care of it. We gaze into each other's eyes with instinctive understanding and familiar longing.

He pulls me into the house. Kissing me greedily, he backs me all the way into the bedroom. Beneath my soft cotton gypsy blouse he fondles my breasts.

"No bra. Mmmm. Baby, how you gonna do that to me?"

"You know I don't need one, especially au naturelle in my own garden."

"Yeah, I laid my eyes on those treats." He nuzzles those treats with his nose. "But damn girl, I'm not the only guy driving by here feasting his eyes on you."

"So is this a drive-by?" We laugh. That's exactly what it is.

"It is now. Baby, you know I can't stay away for long anyway, and then I drive by and see you dressed like this. It made me hungry." He licks his lips, lifting my blouse to fill his mouth with my breasts. I pull his t-shirt over his head. My breath catches when I first lay my eyes on his body.

"No panties either?" he breathes into my neck, sliding his hands under my skirt. "Fuck baby, what are you trying to do to me?"

But it's what he does to me that rattles the house and shimmers the stratosphere whenever he's here. He kisses me and windows tremble. He touches me and sparks fly. He caresses me and I am his to do whatever he wishes. He knows how to please. What pleases him, thrills me.

He unzips my cotton skirt and it falls to the floor. I drop his drawers and slide my hands over his hard thick cock. He picks me up like a toy, drops me onto the bed, and laughs. He leans in. He's got that look, the look of a man consumed by desire. He licks his bottom lip. He wants it.

"Come on now baby, open up for me. I need to get back into your sweet stuff, mmmm mmmm mmmm." He commands and I comply with pleasure. I spread my legs and my labia blossom open just for him. I know what he wants to see, we've done this before. I moisten up just thinking about him, but when he starts to kiss me, move on me, do what he does, well let's just say he loves the lube. "Damn, girl."

We won't be taking our time today. He's ready to dive in right now. He's built big and understands he has to move slowly as we begin so I can receive him. I sit up and reach for him. When he has that look, when he points his cock at me, I'm ready to open up and take it in, right now. We blast off.

He devours my mouth, sucking on my lips. He licks my nipples then nestles into my neck. His hands slide from my waist and slip under my back. I'm ravenous for him, I can never get enough. Now his hands are under my ass and pulling me closer. I grasp his hips, guiding his long delicious journey into me. He dips slowly, rhythmically in and out, distributing my wetness along his shaft, setting the pace. Sometimes that's all he has to do to make me come immediately. Because of his size, when he starts to move inside of me, touching every throbbing erotic zone, he sends me quaking over the edge without effort.

This is where we start today, straight over the edge. My pulsing pulls him in deeper and he moans, rolls his eyes and grabs my shoulders. He pushes me back onto the bed, pulls my ass to the edge and lifts me up to reach him, angling my hips for a perfect fit. Pressing his hot hard cock into me, a little more, a little deeper, he gauges the effect of his penetration. He stops and holds there, watching me, testing, teasing, waiting for me to be able to fully receive him. I study his eyes, his face, cherish the little beads of sweat gathering on his brow and upper lip. He smiles that knowing smile and licks his bottom lip again. He knows just what to do to make me go mad with desire.

"Ooooh, sugar. Right there, just like that," I gasp and pull him further into me. Oh yes, he knows. He knows exactly what I want and need. Someday I'll write a song or poem or a long treatise on what he does and how it moves me. At the moment, all I can do is him. He pulls out a little and smiles again. A couple quick shallow pumps before he thrusts into my deep and I reverberate into another orgasm.

"Like this, baby?" he teases. I groan with pleasure. He adjusts me to his movements, his large broad hands holding my ass in place. My slippery cunt, even wide open, is a snug glove fit. "How 'bout this?" He mutters, his breath coming faster, his body leaning over me. I gasp, my body yielding to him, merging with him.

He slows down a little and I hear him whisper, "Baby, fuck, what are you doing? You gonna do that now?"

I wasn't even aware that I had started undulating in synch with him. We have a way of moving together that is guaranteed ecstasy for both of us. When we slip into that dance, one of us has to slow it down or change it up otherwise he'll come sooner than he wants to. I am usually so lost in bliss by this point that I rely on him to make that effort if he wants. But now I can feel him close to the edge too, and I don't want it to end yet. I pull him onto the bed and on top of me.

He slows down and begins to regain control. He lifts himself above me smiling that smile, like he knows my secret. He does. He watches my face and kisses me and I hold onto him for dear life. Sometimes I don't want to be this vulnerable with him and he is aware of this. Sometimes he'll become tender and loving with me, helping me come back around to feel less exposed, less fragile. Today he pauses a moment before encouraging me on. I'm grateful. I know he's trying to hold on for me. "That's right, baby. I got what you want. Go ahead and take it. Take all you can, girl." He allows me to spend myself and still he doesn't shoot. He's holding his own admirably this afternoon. I know him so well sexually, that I can predict where he'll want to go next. "I know what you want, honey." I murmur as he stares into my eyes. "You can have what you want." He withdraws slowly, turning me over, lifting me to my knees. His large hands wrap themselves around my hips and he eases in from behind. He loves to ride me fierce like this, as much as I love mounting him and fucking him to oblivion. We synch into our rhythm, my vagina contracting and milking him. "Damn baby. You gonna do that to me now? Yeah you're doin' that. Oh. Yeah. Do. That. Aaaahh, fuck me!" He seizes my hips and pumps. I'm so opened up now that I can take him on and all the way in. I lose all sense of place and time. Tearing at the sheets, crying out his name like an anthem, I'm lost even to myself. "Oh God baby, yeah, right there now. Hang on." He holds me down and issues a deep throaty groan as he comes deep and full. "Goddamn."

He lets himself go inside of me and I throb in welcoming heat. His hot juice fills me and mixes with mine. I wish I could describe how his jizz feels inside of me. Disclose what it does. Recite how it communicates something crucial and essential to my body, to my being.

His arms circle my waist and he lays on top of me, breathing heavily into my neck. Once we've calmed, he rolls onto his back and I curl into him under his arm, basking in his luscious musky scent. I watch his face. His eyes are closed and he's smiling, licking his bottom lip like he does when he gets what he wants. In these moments I completely and utterly adore him. I touch his cheek and trace his lips with my finger. He doesn't speak, but he turns toward me and looks deeply into my eyes. Then he kisses me tenderly on the lips and cheek before drifting back into his own private world.

He's a former military man with a built-in alarm clock. He could be sound asleep and when it's the designated time, he wakes up fully alert and launches into whatever activity he's planned. I know he isn't asleep now, just relaxing, allowing his body to slowly pull his essence back in. I smooth my hand over his chest and belly then rest it on his cock. It responds to my touch with a familiar little nod. His cock is magnificent. The most beautiful, perfectly functioning unit I have ever known. He's aware of that, of course. He's a big guy with a big dick and he knows how to use it confidently and expertly. The way he uses it to thrill me makes him my decorated hero.

Our bond is our indescribable physical attraction, our sexual compatibility. True, like most women, sometimes I let my imagination wander to a story of us being in love, as if I knew what that was exactly. I'm careful with that. He and I have fantastic sex. What we do together is love expressed physically. Oh, we make plans and spend time doing all kinds of other things together, but an unexpected drive-by booty-call on a beautiful afternoon is a delicious way to wrap the day. I could never refuse. What would be the point?

His inner alarm goes off and he opens his eyes. He rolls over me kissing my breasts and belly before hopping up and into the shower. I continue to luxuriate in the bed, taking pleasure in how sensuous and alive, how content and completely satisfied my body feels. The water's running, he's singing and I'm drifting, when I hear his boisterous laugh.

He calls out to me, "Damn girl, you're one fucking fabulous piece of ass. Baby, I fucking love your sweet ass." He laughs again and so do I. He's made that point clear more than once. Then I hear him mutter to himself, "Damn I love that woman." Then scarcely audible, "Yeah, fuck me, I really love her." Now so quietly it's almost a whisper and I wonder if I'm hearing him right, "Baby, I love you."

I hold my breath, I can't help it. My heart swells with joy. He's never confessed this before. I want to shout that I love him too because I do, if I trust myself to admit the truth. I know he doesn't realize that I heard him, but this is a moment I will hold close and cherish. I blow him a secret kiss. One true thing I know is that he'll drive by again, soon. I trust how much we both love that.

"Women need a reason to have sex. Men just need a place."
~ Billy Crystal

The Car with California Plates

Here we are in the middle of scenic Chelan, Washington's sunny high desert wine country. But why Jennie chose this small crowded campground, at the far end of a tiny algae-splotched lake, is a mystery to me. We arrived just this morning for a four-day taste and tour of the local vineyards. Our two mega-coach condo-like RVs are squeezed end-to-end into a jagged semi-circle on one corner of the grounds like wagons *westward ho!* The savages all around us are college kids with tents and cases of beer on a spring break bender.

Jennie is one of my dearest friends and she arranged this rendezvous so her two closest girl friends from the Midwest and I could get to know each other. They flew out last night and we met in Seattle this morning, then rented these coaches to caravan over the Snoqualmie Pass with Jennie's car in tow. Now we're based at this camp for a long weekend of girls-on-wine time. They are here to drink and so are the kids. I am here primarily because of gorgeous pictures and enticing articles I've seen in trendy Northwest magazines describing romantic trips to the wine county. When Jennie suggested this trip, I assumed that she meant the Washington State wine country around Walla Walla and Prosser, where vintners, wine makers and chefs have created a world-class destination for tasting and touring. I hadn't realized that the apple growers in Chelan were now planting every craggy hillside and spare inch of space near their orchards with grapes too.

We've just returned from an afternoon of touring, tasting and buying wine and I already have a wine headache. We're quite a ways out from town and are definitely the seniors camped here. We have three more days.

At sunset the grounds fill up with campfires, pounding music, boisterous laughter, engine-revving cars cruising in and out, scantily clad girls parading back and forth before clusters of loud preening muscle-bound guys. Leaning against the gate are three burly cops on duty. It's the three cops who capture my attention and I'm wondering why this little campground would require their presence. When I ask, one tells me they hire on every year at this time to keep order. My romantic wine-country notions don't reconcile easily with this news.

I can't help being amused though as I watch these kids, clutching their beverages, sizing each other up. These are scenes reminiscent of another time and place. On this evening I'm not one of them. I'm an observer, a social scientist, a displaced parental unit camped on the wrong weekend in the wrong era. The energy and excitement are escalating as the campers gear up for a rowdy evening. Three cops and a squad car don't seem to be able to put a damper on that.

One reserved campsite, just in front of us on the lakeside, is still vacant. This pleases me because I have an unobstructed view of the lake, such as it is, from where I've positioned my chair around our fire pit. But this is a momentary pleasure. A car with California plates pulls up and three tall handsome black guys spill out. One is about 35, and the other two appear to be twins, I'd guess in their 20s. They quickly and efficiently set up their camp and within minutes have a large tent erected, fire started, chairs set around it, music thumping and beers in their hands.

We acknowledge each other with nods. I note that they have all kinds of stuff with them including floats, several coolers, a football, Frisbee, fishing gear and a slalom water ski. I absently wonder what they might be noticing as they occasionally glance this way. Here sits a group of decidedly older white women. This one in particular is wrapped in a velvet shawl, sipping a glass of white wine in front of a duplex of gigantic motor homes. This is an image I find both alarming and comical. I have to laugh.

We ladies turn in early as the party gears up. Later, and all through the night, there's chaos outside the walls of the RVs. The ambient track of ocean waves on my iPod covers the rowdy noise out there and I'm able to catch a decent sleep. By morning the drunken enthusiasm has subdued to the gaiety of a wicked hangover, but I'm awake and refreshed. The sun is shining through the blinds, calling me to enjoy it with a coffee at the end of the dock. The thought of a little space alone before we launch into a full day of touring is appealing.

Jennie is still sleeping soundly with the aid of her eye mask and earplugs. While my coffee brews, I pull on my hoodie and step out of the rig to stretch in the early sun. I'm just in time to witness two of the cops shove a kid into the squad car and spin out of the gate.

"What the bloody hell?" I comment to no one in particular. I hadn't expected anyone to be up yet . . . or still.

The guys with the California plates are sitting at their fire as if they had never moved. One apparently heard me. Yawning, he begins to describe how an annoying kid was tripping all night, had tried unsuccessfully to start several fights and this morning smacked his girl. The cops are finally hauling him off. My fading fantasy and now my morning reverie are going up in smoke like the smoldering embers of last night's campfires. I survey the camp. Kids are passed out on the grass, feet are sticking out of tents, empty bottles are thrown everywhere. The lone cop is leaning against a tree, and I am wishing I were anywhere but here. Last night when I asked Jennie why she reserved a site in a place like this, she explained that it was the only camp left on this weekend that could accommodate our rigs. I wonder if she's oblivious to how weird and incongruent it is for us with our giant coaches to be in the midst of this party. I am now also wondering how I am going to deal with three more days of it. I am about to find out.

"Hey pretty lady, you're lookin' real fine this morning in those jammies and that hoodie." It's one of the twins from the car with California plates. I give him a long look. He shifts the brim of his cap to the back of his head and grins, "Oh, I'm sorry, did I offend you?" This provokes quiet chuckles from all three of them. We lock eyes with a mutual degree of attitude. I shrug nonchalantly then turn and step back into the coach to check my coffee. This isn't the first time a young black guy has hit on me recently but I'm at a loss to explain why. I close the door quietly and find myself grinning in amusement. That simple physical response automatically lightens my mood with an unanticipated feeling of excitement. A thought flits across my mind. My wine country weekend might include the possibility of becoming even more entertaining. My imagination is captured before my better judgment is able to quash it.

I pour a steaming mug, grab my phone and a low chair, and head to the end of the dock. The camp smolders at my back and the lake and hills sparkle with dew before me. The morning sun is already warm and it feels wonderful to peel off my sweatshirt and bask in it. I'm gratefully alone with the stillness, momentarily forgetting about the crowded mess behind me. In this early morning light the terrain around this little lake, with the colors of the grape-covered hillsides directly across, is more beautiful than I had noticed before. It's quiet. I take a deep breath and relax.

But it isn't long before Jamz—yes, he tells me his name is Jamz with a Z—strolls down the dock to join me. Unannounced and uninvited, he sits just a little too close. More than joining me, he immediately moves on me.

"I could sure use some coffee this morning," he offers as a greeting. Interrupted from the pleasure of my quiet space, I am

73

not amused and offer him another long silent look. "Would you like to make me some or share yours?"

"No and no." I'm annoyed but I can't help noticing that he has dark serious eyes, a beautiful toned body and a cocky grin, which triggers an un-beckoned visit from my earlier fleeting thought of alternative weekend entertainment. "This place is teeming with semi-naked girls in case you failed to notice. The action is all behind us dude. Why are you down here sitting way too close and bothering me?"

"I want your attention and you have some coffee."

"You're bothering me."

"Maybe you could get used to it."

"I'm not getting up to make you coffee and I'm not sharing mine. I'm confident that whatever it is you really want you can find it up at one of those campsites."

"Don't try to pimp me to one of those girls up there. It won't work. They're all the same. There's something about you that interests me."

"Besides coffee, what might that be?" I can't help noticing that I'm shifting from being annoyed to mildly amused which should be sounding my alarm. It isn't. He's young and he already has a way; commanding, charming and charismatic. "How old are you?" I ask him.

"Why does that matter? I don't care how old you are. I can see that you're hot for whatever your age is, but since you ask, I'm 26."

He's younger than two of my children! I feel compelled to clear up any wild assumptions he might be having about me or what I can do for him. "Listen, Jamz with a Z, not only is that huge RV I'm traveling in not mine, I am not a waitress nor a bank and I have children your age. I can think of no relevant reason for you to be coming onto me in this way."

"Why do you have to insult me? Do you think that will put me off? It won't. I saw how you kept looking over at our camp last night. What's your name? I want to get to know you. I told you, you're the only woman here that interests me."

"Are you studying acting?" I ask. He laughs and admits that yes, he is. I thought so.

"Come on. I can tell you're interested in me too. You can't hide it. What's your name."

Now I have to laugh. What is it about me that makes men think I'm interested in them before I even notice that I might be? I haven't even been my usual open friendly self with this kid. But then he purposefully places his hand on my knee and this is how it happens. Electrical and chemical impulses course between us and an indefinable connection is sparked. It's something that you can't with all your might make happen, and when it does, you can't make it not happen. That it's happening here and now with him can only mean trouble, or I am shocked by the sudden unsolicited thought: delicious fun. Good grief. "My name is Savannah."

We sit now in a heightened awareness of each other. Since he is an aspiring actor I'm convinced the bits of his story he's sharing are a twisted, trumped up and sanitized version of the truth and tell him so. He smiles broadly, ignoring my observation, then proceeds to ask me intensely personal questions.

"Where's your man?"

"None of your business."

"When was the last time you made love with him?"

"Are you serious? What makes you think you can ask me a question like that? You can't. I have no intention of engaging with you on a personal level."

"I feel you," he whispers, moving closer.

"You know nothing about me. Back off."

"I know that you're beautiful, and I want to know you better. You won't be able to resist me for long, Ms. Savannah."

"We'll see."

His energy is charged. He moves closer still and as he does his knees fall open and I see the contour of his cock through his nylon basketball shorts. Involuntarily, certain juicy parts of my anatomy begin to tingle and I prudently clamp my knees together. Lusty curiosity strains to get the best of me, forever my damn downfall.

Just two weeks ago I returned from a rendezvous with a man I've been interested in. As our budding relationship deepened, I imagined him a possible partner and hoped in time, a more interesting and ardent lover. I entertained the idea of that long-distance romance for many reasons of easy compatibility, not the least of which being that we're the same age. Unfortunately, he does not stir my juices nearly as much as he originally stimulated my mind. I had just been reflecting on my growing disappointment about the direction that love affair was headed when Jamz landed next to me on the dock. Apparently those frustrating reflections left me vulnerable to this young one's sensual overtures.

"You've been disappointed in your lover recently, haven't you? I think you need some sexual healing," he croons in a low throaty voice, caressing my cheek, brushing my hair behind my ear. "I'd like to do something about that."

I feel like I've just been ambushed or dropped into a scene from a B movie. "What would make you think that?" I can't believe I've allowed him this kind of access to me. "Go away. I came down here for some space."

"I told you, I feel you." Laughing now, he stands up and towers over me. The distinct definition of his generous cock protruding through his white shorts engulfs my formally serene view, penetrating my imagination. A flood of erotic hormones course through my body without my permission. Damn it. "What's the problem? Are you worried what your friends will think if they see us together like this?"

"Us together like what? And worried about what they will think? What about what I think?" I'm beginning to recognize myself in him. We're alike in this way; we sense something, weave a compelling story around it, then believe it's true. Sometimes it's not, but when it presents something we think we want and getting it seems feasible, action will be taken.

"What do you think? What's the problem? Are you racist?"

"Sit down, damn it," I demand. I can't think clearly with his sex hovering over me like that. He drops down and sits scowling, crossing his arms over his chest. "Look Jamz with a Z. Yes I do have a problem with the idea of the two of us together, whatever the hell you mean by that. Race, however, is not my issue. My issue, in your case, is the obvious fact of the chasm in our ages. It's also the fact that you are playing me so blatantly and conspicuously. Knock it off! Why are you pursuing me? Is this your idea of sport this morning or are you still drunk?"

He rolls onto his back, arms still crossed over his chest howling with laughter. Even though I'm completely pissed off I can't help catching his contagion and start laughing too. I push against his shoulder, shoving him away from me. With his legs in the air, the tip of his distracting protrusion peeks out from his shorts. I can't take my eyes off of it and am beginning to forget why I am so annoyed. "Why are you laughing, damn it."

"Because you've got fire, beautiful woman, and it's turning me on. I may be bothering you but you aren't intimidated by me. I know you aren't racist. My radar told me that. But I'm hurt that you think just because I am younger than you, I'm not worthy of your affection."

"You're hurt? Nice acting, Hollywood."

"Hey, stop insulting me just because I want us to get together. I don't give up that easily. I'm not going away."

"Until 20 minutes ago there was no concept of us together."

Jamz just smiles and nods, "Now there is."

This young man is persistent. He's already a skilled player; studying acting will make him a pro. While he pursues that craft, he could do well in sales. He's obviously used to getting his own way. I have no idea why he is trying to lure me and while I'll admit

I'm flattered and even enticed, I'm also uncomfortable and feel foolish. I sigh deeply. What the hell is happening here?

"My brother, cousin and I are going water skiing on the main lake for the day. Then we're going to party in town. When we get back I want you to join me at our fire. I'm going to fix a place for us to lie together away from everyone else."

"Lie together? Are you completely insane?" He pulls me close, and before I can respond, he runs his fingers through my tangled hair and kisses me lightly on both cheeks, his lips lingering on mine briefly. I'm caught off guard and pull away, but not before I register how long I hesitated. "Stop it. Now. I'm not playing this game with you."

"I'm not gaming you, Ms. Savannah. I want to see you later and maybe you don't realize it yet, but you'll want to see me, too. By the end of this day you'll have thought it over and decided we're fresh and should be lying together tonight. So it's settled."

"It is not settled." Jamz has luscious lips, beautiful hands, a tall slim toned body. His eyes are dark and sensuous and difficult to read, compelling. He's intense, a Scorpio, dangerous. He is dangerous for me and I recognize that. It is not settled.

Jennie calls me up to the campsite for breakfast. I wave to her and start gathering my things. Jamz grabs my arm to stop me. "Don't you want to be with me, even just a little? Why are you trying to act like you don't? Why are you putting up so much resistance? We're both here. Why can't we just enjoy each other?"

The answers to those three questions have become blatantly obvious to me. I am putting up this rather feeble resistance because: (a) yes, I do want to be with him, just a little, damn it (b) I don't know why the hell I'm even talking to him let alone starting to like him, and (c) because I must resist, I absolutely must.

"Look, I am very flattered by your attention, but just because we are both here at this camp at the same time doesn't mean we are meant to be together. I can't even begin to imagine that scenario." That statement, I realize immediately, is in danger of becoming a lie and he senses it.

"You're not a very good liar. I want to make love with you, and I could feel you turn on. You want me, too." His serious dark brown eyes are mischievous now and I have to laugh. My intention to make it a dismissive laugh fails. As we part, he calls after me, "See ya later, baby." I shake my head. That possibility of alternative entertainment this weekend? It's now setting up camp in my imagination. My better judgment has apparently packed up and gone home.

Over breakfast my new girlfriends press me for information. Laughing, I defer their inquiries and offer them the idea that he was dared to come onto me with cash riding on the wager back at his camp. That could very well be true.

Jennie asks, "Well . . . did he win?" I tilt my head quizzically. "Well, he obviously succeeded in coming onto you, so what else, beside the wager, has he won?"

"Very funny, Jenn." I laugh, but a deep internal blush is slowly spreading through me and the idea of a deliciously unanticipated possibility is taking hold in my body. All through the afternoon, traipsing behind the girls, my mind is not on the vines. No matter how many silent admonishing conversations I have with myself, this young homeboy player has turned me on and it's fun and it's embarrassing and it's ridiculous.

Our gang returns to the campground after a long day of touring, tasting and a wonderful dinner at a nearby chateau. It's dark now and the party atmosphere is revving up with loud music and a repeat of the last night's parade of beer-swilling kids making their rounds from camp to camp. Around our fire, wrapped in our shawls, we ladies are a bit tipsy but continue to sample more of the wonderful wines we purchased today. I can't restrain myself from glancing towards the lakeside camp in front of us. The guys are getting ready to take off for town again.

I'm startled when Jamz boldly calls to me, insisting that I walk with him for a minute. I'm anxious and flustered as he wraps his arm around my waist, leading me away from the fire-light. I step away from his embrace immediately, nearly melting where he touched me. I have to put some distance between us because Jennie's incredulous glare is burning a hole in the back of my brain.

"My brother and cousin are staying in town tonight so you can sleep in my tent with me when I get back." He declares, circling my waist again, his touch informing me how seductive and thrilling a night with him could be.

"Okay, Jamz. Listen carefully, please. I want you to understand this because I'm explaining it for the last time. I am not staying with you. That is not even a remote possibility." I am rue-fully aware that my body is not paying the least bit of attention to my words. Neither is Jamz.

"Yes, it is," he insists, blowing me a kiss as he jumps into the waiting car with California plates. We've reached détente.

The rest of the evening I sit by the fire, chatting with the girls about nothing that matters, drinking more wine and strug-gling to convince myself that I meant what I said to Jamz. My new girlfriends think this little escapade with him is a harmless amusement. Jennie does not. She knows me and my proclivities for amorous adventures and her side comments and body lan-guage have made that abundantly clear. Eventually I'm able to get a grip on myself, forcibly upgrade my standards of behavior and retire into the coach to escape the endless chatter and wine around our campfire and the chaos brewing in the rest of the camp. All through the night, delicious thoughts of Jamz weave through my tangle of dreams.

In the morning, after a much less raucous night out there than the one before, I emerge into the early sun again to see him sitting alone by the embers of his fire, holding his head. He waves me over, shielding his eyes from the sun. He's angry. "I waited up all night for you. Why are you acting like you don't care about me? You hurt my feelings."

"What the hell? What do you think is happening here? Did you not hear or understand anything I told you last night?" I don't know what to make of this boy. I sit down and attempt to convince him one last time that he has mistaken my friendliness for something more.

"I know the truth, and so do you." He croaks as he crawls into his tent to sulk and sleep off his hangover. I'm left sitting alone with my own throbbing head, as I gaze out across the lake and contemplate this disconcerting scenario. He's right. He's un-relentingly authentically correct about the truth. And I am not. A quick review of Jamz starring in my erotic dreams all night confirms this. Nevertheless, I have to end this tempting seduction now. I glance around the ruins of last night's party. My friends are starting to stir within their rigs. I smell coffee brewing and get up to join the girls for breakfast. I peek in on Jamz, curled up and asleep in his tent. I could have been curled up next to him there this morning after a night of real time erotica. Just knowing that he was a sweet possibility makes me smile and brings me a sense of pleasure and also relief. So that's that.

I also know I have to pass on another day of touring. I cannot consume another ounce of wine, and have no desire to keep up with them today. I need a reprieve and some time alone to clear my head. I let the girls know that I'll be joining them for dinner later. Waving them off to drink more wine, eat more food and buy more stuff, I'm grateful for the relative quiet at Camp Hangover. Most of the kids are either stretched out in their tents or sitting at picnic tables staring blankly at the lake.

I head to the dock to nap in the sun. Lying on my mat absorbing the warmth, I'm lulled by the lapping water against the sides. I hadn't realized I was holding so much tension in my body and drift into a light dreamy sleep. Much later, I awaken thirsty and hungry and decide to go back in for a bite of lunch. I'm drying off after a refreshing shower when I hear knocking on the locked door. Jennie must have decided to return early. I wrap the towel around me and open the door for her.

But it's Jamz, revived and grinning. He steps in without invitation, pulls me to him and undrapes my towel before I can react.

"Yeah, I like that!" He licks his lips, staring at my freshly waxed bikini line. I pull away from him in shock and muster enough presence of mind to close and lock the door. Apparently I have just enough presence of mind left to realize that I'm losing it.

"Can I take a shower too?" Without waiting for an answer, he slowly strips in front of me daring me to avert my eyes. I can't. He showers quickly, sauntering back out still wet, catching me as I'm slipping into my dress. He pulls me into his damp naked, and now I can't help noticing, very aroused body. I feel myself succumbing. I can't help that either.

He unzips my dress and brushes the straps off my shoulders. It drops to the floor. One hand slides over my ass and pulls down my panties. While he nuzzles my neck, his other hand stealthily slips between my thighs. His exploring fingers expertly locate my on button with exactly the right pressure, exactly the right friction. My insides clench and I tremble, grasping his shoulders to hold myself steady. Somewhere within the recesses of my lost mind a thought is shouting, urging me to stop. Stop this now. My body turns a deaf ear and ignores it, viscerally remembering him like this from last night's dreams. I am unable to resist his touch. Apparently I've also become mute.

Jamz is grinning. Clearly, he has all the power, has read me accurately and is enjoying that. Whatever resolve I thought I'd mustered last night has evaporated with his touch this morning. Picking me up like a baby, he strolls effortlessly across the room to the bed, kissing and nuzzling the curve of my neck, one of my weaknesses. How does he instinctively know that? He lays me back hovering over me, his hard cock insinuating itself between my thighs. Burying his head between my breasts, one hand firmly grasps my ass as the other delves deep and explores my inner sanctum. I clutch him. I want him. I need it and pull him to me, my pelvis thrusting, opening to receive him. His middle finger discovers my spot with just the right pressure and I'm done in and pull him to me.

Rather than entering me, he grasps my hips and goes down on me voraciously. I come apart completely, sensually over-whelmed. He knows exactly what to do and another thought flits across my mind. He's so young and so sexually savvy; he's already a pro. What does this mean? I'm unable to hold this or any thought. Lost in an orgasmic paradise, I come. I try again to pull him to me. I want him inside of me. I find my voice now and beg him but instead he spreads my legs wide and watches. I can't stop now. My body undulates as cum issues from my depths. I can feel it. I've never been witnessed like this before. It unsettles me, thrills me. I open my eyes and see him smil-ing, licking his lips. Closing them again, I dissolve moaning in pleasure.

He takes my face in his hands forcing me to look into his eyes. I don't want to. He insists, expecting me to comply, holding my gaze. "You've wanted to make those sounds for a long time haven't you, baby? You've wanted to open up. You wanted some-one who could make your juicy pink places slippery and wet. I knew you wanted it. You want me, you can't deny that now."

I close my eyes again. I can't believe he's talking to me this way. No one talks to me like that. I feel vulnerable. I've complete-ly succumbed to him and feel as if I'm losing my sovereignty. When I open my eyes again, I see he's still smiling. When I finally begin to get a grip on myself, I whisper, "you're quite gifted, Jamz with a Z and I see that you are . . . uh . . . primed and ready." He kisses my lips then dips down and licks my clit again. "You must want it too."

"Woman! What have I been trying to tell you?"

"Condom?" He produces one out of nowhere and hands it to me grinning.

"A magician." I giggle and rip it open. He closes his eyes and holds his breath while I roll it slowly down his shaft, then guide his entry into me. I feel my dominion returning.

We move together in a dream-like state, slowly finding a rhythm. I want to kiss him. I want his lips. Our eyes fix on each other. I arch my back offering my mouth to him. We connect, we bond, our tongues seeking and finding, our mouths devouring, ravishing. He pushes himself deeper and I contract around him, a million little pulses rippling outward through my body to my fingers and toes. I am completely immersed in the pleasure he brings me.

Urgency overtakes him. He's so deeply enveloped within me that his thrusting mushroom tip reverberates against my cervix. Groaning my name into my neck, between my breasts, pumping, frenzied, he startles me when he shouts, "Now! Now!" Exploding into me, I ripple into an equal explosion of my own. His power rocks me, rocks us both intensely and long after our climax is spent, we lay vibrating together until the room stops swirling.

He doesn't pull out. We lay silently in each other's arms for a long luxurious time. As I slowly become more present it dawns on me that Jennie could return at any moment. I'm not thrilled about the prospect of being discovered in her rig, on her bed with Jamz, and this rogue thrill of forbidden pleasure becomes tinged with anxiety.

I am still filled with him, and he is making no effort to move. If I hadn't had such an interrupting thought I wouldn't want him to, but the thought returns. I express my concern to him. He doesn't share it. He's propped on his elbow now, still inside of me holding me close with his other arm and staring at me. "Let's get up," I plead. I have no idea what time it is, and the anxiety of Jennie finding me here with him like this has thrust me back into our pre-coital reality. I'm determined that he get up and go. I try to push him off. He won't budge. I encourage him to get up and take a shower. I offer to make some lunch.

"I like it here inside of you. I'm not hungry. I'm not moving."

"Please?" I beg him for mercy, to think for a minute about what it would mean to have my friends walk in on us. This makes him laugh. I twist and squirm to get free of him but that only serves to arouse him and I feel him getting hard inside of me again.

"Thanks baby, that's good. Yeah, you're really good. Let's not waste this." He chuckles and starts to move again, his cock touching every now ultra-sensitive part of me. My body responds against my will, overriding my concerns yet again. I try in vain to resist him. "That's right, woman. You keep moving like that. We're gonna do this again like I knew we were meant to." I give in, I can't help myself. His insistence thrills me. When he pulls out for a second I'm disoriented. He flips me over quickly and enters me from behind, adjusting me to a perfect angle, into a perfect fit. "Bang bang!" He shouts, throbbing against my spot sending me over the edge. I cry out in the most intense orgasm I've had in years. He blasts the rest of what he has into me with such force that we both collapse. He's on top of me, panting and holding me so tight I can't move. I can't remember why I want to.

We lay motionless, thoughtless, as if suspended in time. Our breathing synchronizes and quiets, seduced by the sensation of drifting in and out of consciousness. It is he who finally withdraws and moves to sit up, pulling me up with him. Wrapping his legs around me and pulling mine around him, we sit face to face. Holding both my hands in his, we gaze silently into each other's eyes. Stroking my cheek, he says softly, "Damn, woman. You surprised me." I'm without words, but then he adds, "And now I see how this is gonna go down with you." He unwraps himself from me. "Okay, you're right baby, let's get up so you don't have to stress about your friend coming here." He's being tender with me. "I know that would be hard on you." I nod, grateful to hear him say this. "I see that you like it hard, though. I'll make sure you get enough of that from now on." He rolls over the bed laughing. I'm still speechless, stunned by an unexpected wave of affection I am feeling for him in this moment.

I watch him dress taking a long appreciative look at him, his body, his face, his energy, which has changed and softened dramatically. He smiles and bends to kiss my forehead and I realize, as if awakening from a dream, that he's leaving. This is what needs to happen right now, isn't it? Isn't this what I want? He grabs two apples from a bowl on the table, throws one to me, munching his happily while he finishes dressing. I slip on my dress and stand there in confusion, apple in hand, this surreal experience with Jamz sinking in, exerting itself into my reality.

Before he leaves he tells me that he and the guys will be packing up and hitting the road before dark. This news distresses me, adding to my confused and conflicted emotions about him and what we've just done together. Watching him put his number in my phone and mine in his seems somehow natural and ordinary. Then he kisses me goodbye, a long deep sensitive kiss. I am still unable to speak, my feelings overwhelming any ability to express myself. I think I am hearing him say that he'll be seeing me again soon since he goes back and forth between our two neighboring cities all summer, but this makes no sense to me. He couldn't be talking about us.

"You're my woman now, Ms. Savannah." His rowdy laughter and dramatic declaration rouse me from my blissed-out stupor and there is nothing to do but join him. I have to laugh. I can hardly contain myself and laugh until tears are rolling down my cheeks. I have just fucked this very confident, very young dude who's breaking it all down for me. I can't think past the last two insane hours, let alone begin to imagine planning into a future that contains an us.

We kiss goodbye a last time and he slaps my ass shouting, "That's all mine now!" Then he steps out of the coach, slamming the door behind him and just like that, he's gone.

I stare at the door stunned, apple still in hand, unable to move from the spot where he left me. The imprint of his lips on mine just now, visceral. The damp swelling between my legs, delectable. I'm bathed in a conflux of confusing and delicious feelings. Absently, I take a bite of my apple and smile. It's the sweetest, juiciest, crunchiest I've ever tasted.

Eventually, I gaze around the coach realizing where I am and reflect on how I've just spent the afternoon. I find my panties, slip them on, smooth out the bed and collapse back onto it. My body feels rejuvenated and alive and I want to relish that. My face seems to have adopted a permanent smile. By the time the girls return to pick me up for dinner, I am relaxed, dressed to go and ravenous.

As we turn out of the camp, I notice that at least half of the kids, tents and cars are gone, including Jamz and his crew. I can't take my eyes off the site where that car with the California plates had been parked. Nor can I pause the movie in my mind, playing out the luscious details of my spontaneous spring break adventure. The slightest hint of his scent lingers on me and I tingle all over as my mind replays this afternoon's secret delight.

(Postscript surprise: The story doesn't end there. As spring gave way to summer, we slipped in and out of each other's lives and bodies in the most tantalizing and tasty ways until one morning in early fall, just before he headed back to school in California. We made love one last tender time. As I kissed him goodbye and sent him on his way, I told him he was one for the books. "I expect you to write one, Ms. Savannah. Dedicate it to me and I'll star in the movie someday.")

This story is dedicated to Jamz with a Z,
my homeboy with the California plates.

"What you seek is seeking you."
  ~ Rumi

That Thing!

W hat is the nature of *That Thing!*? How does it express itself? *That Thing!* simply exists or it does not. It's an unexplainable magnetic attraction that connects people. It goes beyond being merely interested. It's magical and luscious. Acknowledging the presence of *That Thing!* is pleasure enough. It has a frequency, a signal that people immediately recognize and resonate with. It embeds itself into their interactions. When it's present between me and a man, it will always register on my radar and capture my full attention. It's delightful and it's irresistible. It can't always be acted upon, but when it can, I will.

I'm thinking about that time, a couple years ago, when I met Finn. I was visiting my dear friend Milo at his home in Las Sirenas. We gave Finn a lift to the airport and although he and Milo have been business partners and friends for some time, he and I had never met before. We had heat the minute we laid eyes on each other. In that 40-minute ride up to Puerto Vallarta, I learned enough about him to provoke a juicy possibility for half a year. Our short close encounter was a delicious surprise. Finn and I talked and flirted while Milo navigated all those dangerous curves from the village to the city. We all but forgot that Milo was with us. I learned that Finn was smart, quick-witted, into pop culture and all kinds of music. He leaned my way politically, had a contagious easy laugh, was in good shape and pretty dang cute for a middle-aged guy. I liked the way he looked and felt. Although not exactly handsome, his lively blue-grey eyes and short buzzed blonde hair gave him a youthful demeanor. And he had an air of alert intensity I find appealing. Any of these attributes might be enough to hold my interest for a little while, but my antenna registered *That Thing!* and the signal embedded itself.

During the next six months, when Milo called and Finn's name came up, I listened with increased interest. Milo teased me about Finn's many inquiries regarding me. I realized that we had each registered *That Thing!* and were storing a little bit of *what if* in the back of our minds.

When I knew I would be traveling for a business conference, I called Milo and told him that I wanted to add a week on the end of my trip to stay with him at his place in the lush tropical village of Las Sirenas before he headed back north and home for Christmas.

By that time I had already been traveling for two weeks. My best friend and I had spent a week together at a wonderfully rustic B&B in Santa Fe, experiencing New Mexico. The last week however, we were immersed in an intense professional marketing workshop in Albuquerque. Afterwards she returned home and I headed south over the border. I was ready to lavish in some Las Sirenas magic. I couldn't wait to kick back at that curve of beach known for sightings of the mythical mermaids it was named for.

Milo was in fine humor when he picked me up at the airport and I was delighted to hear that he had arranged for dinner at one of my favorite cafés, a sand bar right on the shore. Exhausted from the workshop and traveling, hot and sticky from the drive out to Las Sirenas, nothing sounded better to me at that moment than an ice-cold cerveza. I couldn't wait to lift my skirt and step into the surf. Cervezas on ice, the ocean breeze and Milo's friends were waiting for us. So was Finn.

The warm friendly reception I received from people I see briefly only twice a year was remarkable. They smothered me in hugs, kisses and instant community. Part of it, I came to understand, was that Milo had been sharing various stories of how our two lives had intersected through the years. His ex-pat friends, like him, have places in this little town. Apparently they felt as if they knew me well. That, and from the looks of things, they'd also been enjoying drinks on the beach for a couple of hours.

Finn and I shared a greeting and a shy smile. He was the last to embrace me. When he did, his energy and touch suggested to me that we were riding the same wave. The thermostat of the evening flipped up a notch. During dinner and amid the ani-mated conversations around the table, I purposely did not focus my attention on him. Each time we glanced at one another, *That Thing!* asserted itself, forcing me to adjust myself. He appeared to be having the same struggle. It was fun. My intuition warned me that Finn's interest in me was not exactly a secret from his friends. The intrigue of keeping our sizzle on a low flame generated even more amusement for me. Milo took off to meet another friend as the sun set, so Finn offered to walk me back to Milo's tiny guest casita, my quarters when I'm here with him.

We detoured down the beach reveling in the beauty of the sunset. The dimming light intensified the magnificent colors in the sky. Finn took my hand as we strolled leisurely along the shore. He laughed when I told him how my friend and I had felt drunk and silly from the altitude in Santa Fe, getting lost and turned around on every corner. Finn released my hand and slid his arm around my waist, conveying an unmistakable mes-sage of sensuality. I felt certain that we would be getting to know each other quite a lot better. With only a week here, I hoped that meant soon. Once away from the lights of the cafés and bars, we stopped and embraced. He pulled me to him with such urgency, kissing me so fiercely that my body sensed the future of our story unfolding in rapid and delicious detail.

"I knew it!" I exclaimed breathlessly.

"So did I," he whispered excitedly. "I haven't been able to get you off my mind for all these months, not that I've wanted to. I imagined kissing you and . . ." He stopped mid-sentence, looked into my eyes with deliberate intention and kissed me ravenously. A rogue wave rushed in, drenching me to mid-thigh, leaving my skirt plastered to my legs. For a moment I thought I heard splashes of laughter coming from the dusky foam and strained to see who might be enjoying an evening swim. I noticed a glimmering tail fin as it slipped into the sea and disappeared from sight. Unusual for such a large fish to be this close to shore, I thought. But Finn's enthusiasm was so compelling, my attention was again captured in his embrace. "God, I can hardly contain myself," he laughed.

"I see that, and what's more, I'd like to encourage it." I giggled. *That Thing!* tripped its breaker and began rewiring our circuits.

I pulled away a bit to yank my wet skirt loose from my legs. He stepped closer and slowly slipped his hand under my skirt and caressed my thigh. Again I heard giggles bubbling onto the shore, but when I tried to discern their source I could see nothing.

"I need to touch you," he whispered into my ear before sliding his lips down my neck and nibbling my shoulder. I'd imagined his kisses and much more, so not only did I not resist, I welcomed the sublime sensations coursing through my body. But then, without preamble, his fingers slid under my panties and into me. Within seconds I was trembling to his touch, weak and shivering in the hot, humid evening.

"Oh!" I gasped. I hadn't expected that.

"God. I don't know what got into me. I'm sorry." He stepped away from me, obviously distressed.

I pondered the situation for a moment. What should I do about such an impulsive and immediate coupling? I couldn't suppress a knowing smile. I reached for him, took his face in my hands and kissed him like I meant it. I definitely meant it.

"Don't be sorry. I'm not. The truth is I'm delightfully surprised, aren't you? Isn't it marvelous to meet and connect like this? We both hoped this would happen. We could have fun getting to know each other more thoroughly this week." I wrapped my arms around his neck and pressed my body into him. He slipped his hands up under the back of my shirt and pulled me closer still. A prominent part of his anatomy pointedly indicated that he was ready to start right now.

Several tourists strolling down the beach smiled as they passed and tried to ignore our obvious tryst. An old man leaning against one of the beached outriggers chuckled softly. We hadn't noticed him watching us and decided to move further down the beach. In the gathering darkness, we found a fairly secluded spot sheltered by a weathered palapa with an old overturned boat under it. Finn pulled me down close to him in the sand and we leaned back against the boat, silently watching the gentle surf roll in.

A soft breeze rustled the palm branches that served as the roof of our shelter. The gentle zephyr blew through my hair and refreshed me, but I was hot. The sexual tension between us made me feel like I could spontaneously combust with just his arm around me. I could have fucked him right then, right there in the sand. I took a deep breath, resolutely calming myself. I tried to think about what was happening, what I was doing. Oh, I was thinking about it, for sure, but should I act on it? When *That Thing!* asserts itself in me, I'm incorrigibly compelled to act.

"What should we do, Savannah? What do you want to do?" I considered his strange and somewhat early question, and realized that he had no idea who he was talking to.

"I know exactly what I want to do. We have this yummy possibility. I don't have to think about what to do with that. But listen Finn, I get the impression that you don't want anyone to see us together like this or make assumptions about us. Am I reading that right? Maybe you should tell me what's up so I don't make assumptions either." Again I heard a whisper of laughter on the wind as it caressed my cheek. He was pensive and when he spoke and I was surprised when his voice cracked with emotion.

"I'm not free. My wife and I don't live together but it's still a complicated situation." I already knew that. Milo had told me the whole story, but what did it have to do with us in this intimate moment?

"I guess I might have thought you'd worked that out for yourself. I see that you're happy living here south of the border. You obviously enjoy playing gringo inn-keeper. You may not be free but you seem rather skilled at pretending you are." Milo told me he and his wife have an arrangement that seems to work, at least for him. She doesn't appear to be involved in his community here.

"Something about this little village inspires its inhabitants to indulge in gossip. My wife rarely visits. She doesn't care for the heat, the food or the inconveniences that I love about this place. But she has made several acquaintances here. Unnecessarily compromising her or us is my only concern."

"I'm a once- or twice-a-year visitor with no plans or claims and I certainly have no desire to disrupt your life or my own," I told him.

Maybe he's never had to reconcile the overwhelming power of *That Thing!* with the details of his life, like I have. The fact that he lives down here most of the year alone with a continual stream of beautiful women vacationing, makes me question that. Surely, this isn't the first time he's experienced *That Thing!* He began to explain his situation, a story about family, commitments and finances too complex to unravel.

"I have my own story and complications," I interrupted. That last thing I wanted was to delve into all the difficult details of either of our lives. "We've only begun to discover each other and pleasures neither of us planned. If you're conflicted or feeling guilty already, why are we still sitting here?" No, this wasn't the trajectory I expected or wanted at the moment. I could feel myself sink into a pout and stared out at the tiny sliver of sunset still hanging between the sky and sea. Far on the horizon several objects were bobbing on the swells of ocean. Probably just fishing boats coming in with the day's catch, but I felt as though we were somehow being watched. I imagined *las tres sirenas*, those fabled mischievous temptresses, frolicking in the waves netting us in a seine of moonlight and magic. We were on the verge of ruining the moment. I waited in apprehension. I felt him watching me. Sitting so closely beside him, his arm behind the small of my back, I felt his hesitation now. It was as if we were both held in a point of stillness, unable to move. Was he changing his mind, having a change of heart? Was I? Without a word, he grabbed my shoulders and kissed me with such pressing persuasion that all my own foreboding vanished. Another rogue wave rushed all the way up to our feet as I matched and returned his passion. The sun sank into the depths of the purple horizon.

We could have kissed for hours and that might have been enough except that now I was quivering with desire, yearning for more. I wanted to make love with him. He knew it.

"You're right," he professed at last. "I admit I've thought about being with you, but I didn't really expect it to happen." We pulled each other closer and kissed some more, softer, intimately. "I don't feel guilty, it's not that," he confessed when we came up for air. "I want to learn what's important to you. I want to kiss you till our lips fall off. I want to hold you and make love to you. I want to explore every inch of your body. I want to fuck you. God, now I've said it, but that's the truth. I wasn't expecting to feel this way. I don't know what to do about it, but I want to do something."

"Do what you're doing. Do it some more. I want you to."

The little village of Las Sirenas was alive with La Fiesta de Santa Guadalupe and teeming with both locals and tourists. People of all ages were enjoying the spirited pre-Christmas party with music, dancing and fireworks around the plaza, which left this end of the beach relatively quiet. With those festivities as our backdrop we could have stayed on the beach undetected all night, but why? My tiny casita below Milo's house was nestled in a lush grove of whispering and royal palms. Its private courtyard is secluded with a border of *Higuera arbolitos*, which has become the home of the unblinking, never moving, giant iguana I named Fernando, my personal guardian when I'm here. I wanted to continue our explorations in more privacy and comfort.

We made our way through the crowded plaza with its cacophony of mariachis, church bells and *musica banda*, back up to the house. It was dark, which suggested to me that Milo was either still out or tucked in for the night. We lay outside on the lounges for a little while, talking and kissing some more. I craved his touch. I love to feel this way, though it's uncommon for me to feel this connected so quickly, but what is the explanation for *That Thing!*? There is none. What *That Thing!* demands of me is my full attention and if appropriate, my ardent response. Finn was evoking my most ardent response. I wanted him. I was content to follow his lead, until he proved to have considerably more skill in the art of delayed gratification than I. It was very late. I wanted him to come inside my casita and me.

"Stay with me tonight. Let's make love. I want to sleep in your arms. Please?"

"Milo."

"I can assure you that although Milo may be aware of our attraction, he is merely amused by it. He docsn't care. He won't know we're down here together." Finn was convinced otherwise. He leaned away from me and started to get up but then pulled me close again. I held him tightly. "Don't leave, please."

"Savannah, you are making this impossible for me," he pleaded with a half-hearted laugh, "I think I need to go, and I'm losing my resolve by the second." He kissed me deeply again then untangled my arms from his shoulders. I released him reluctantly, as he adjusted his shorts to hide his bulge. We kissed a final *buenas noches* at the gate with the promise of meeting tomorrow. I was disappointed as I wandered into my casita in a daze but soon realized that without the stimulation of him next to me, I was bushed. In lieu of making love with Finn, a long shower and sleep sounded like the next best thing. Standing in the refreshment of warm water, I thought of his soft lips on mine, the soothing way his hands felt on my flesh, the way his fingers slipped so stealthily inside of me finding my secret spot, my weakness. I reflected on the tone of his voice and that sweet vulnerability he couldn't hide. Once in bed, naked in the steamy heat, I fantasized about how Finn might gratify the yearning in my loins. I hoped it would be soon and wished it was right now. This night's seductive titillation kept me from relaxing until I lost myself in my own pleasuring and drifted to sleep.

I awoke, as if still dreaming, to the unfamiliar sounds of the little village as it roused itself and started about its day. The sun streamed through my bedroom window. Roosters crowed and dogs barked, as I lay tangled in the sheet, disoriented, forgetting where I was. I was startled out of my confusion by Milo first whistling, then shouting loudly for me to wake up and come to the pool for coffee. Wrapping myself in a pareo, I climbed the curved pathway leading to the pool where he had coffee and sliced mangoes waiting.

"Good morning, Milo. It appears I have awakened in heaven, although somewhat earlier than I might have desired." He seemed to be examining me closely, then handed me a steaming mug of dark coffee. "Gracias, mi amor."

"Where did you end up last night, chica? I didn't see you anywhere in town and you weren't here when I came in," he asked, peering over the wire-rimmed glasses hanging precariously on the tip of his nose. Before I could answer he filled a small bowl with fruit, and handing it to me, appraised me expectantly before opening his newspaper.

"Are you my chaperone, sweetie? Where were you? You ditched me, but I can assure you that I've gotten used to fending for myself. I know how to get back here no matter how late it is." We laughed. Milo and I have been close friends since college.

We have an understanding. We don't feel a need to keep watch over each other. "Is there an agenda that I should know about today?"

"Nope, just dinner later with a couple of friends from out of town. I want you to join us, though. I'll be gone most of the day."

"Hmmmm . . . we'll see." I didn't know what this day might bring after last night's intimate delight and I didn't want to encumber myself. I wanted my entire week here to remain open and free from the clock.

"Be ready by six, chica." he called to me, ignoring my vagueness. Then he took off to tend to his various projects.

Alone and feeling decadently lazy, I settled into the hammock, unwrapped my pareo and enjoyed the early sun on my body. The muffled sounds of a mother singing to her child, hens clucking contentedly, men cutting down coconuts before they could fall and a radio crackling Latin ballads lulled me back to sleep. Slowly, as if from a dream, I was awakened by someone kissing my shoulder. Another time or place I might have been startled, but this kiss felt familiar, sensuous and melting. Last night was evolving into today. Finn was kneeling beside me. How long had he been there watching me? I hadn't sensed it. I covered myself and sat up. Settling next to me, he peeled away the wrap to expose one breast. Between tender kisses on my shoulder, neck, cheek and arms, he described how coming upon me sleeping naked in the sun alone had caught him off guard. When he realized that Milo had already left, he wanted to relish the moment, savor it until he couldn't stop himself from touching me.

"Have you had breakfast?" His breath on my neck suggested a more intimate invitation.

I couldn't remember. "I don't think so." I wanted him.

"I'll take you to breakfast."

"Come down to my casita with me and I'll get dressed." I tied my pareo around me, took his hand and led him down the pathway to my quarters. I gestured to the lounges we lay upon last night and introduced him to Fernando. "I'll just take a quick shower and be right out."

While I was still slathering my damp skin with lotion, he came into my room and stood still behind me. Again, I felt his breath on my neck as he slid his hands down my back, smoothing some lotion over my cheeks and down my thighs. I reached for my swimsuit and sundress, but he held my shoulders from behind and turned me toward him.

"Don't get dressed yet," he murmured. "I should have stayed with you last night. What was I thinking?"

There I stood, naked and so close to him I could feel his heat. And he had his hands on me. *That Thing!* overcame me instantly and I reached for him. Taking his face in my hands, I kissed him. He stepped back from me, penetrating me with his energy, his eyes searching and serious. I slipped my hands through his open shirt and around his back, pulling him closer. I was hot, already as hot and humid as the morning. I leaned into him, my naked flesh pressing against him, trembling in the moist heat. His body relaxed against mine, his hand caressed the curve of my neck and shoulder, his lips traveled from my mouth to my breast. I slid my hands slowly down his back and into his shorts and felt his buttocks tighten. He stood straight then and we gazed into each other's eyes for a long moment, then he kissed me on my forehead. Slipping my hands around to his front, I opened the clasp on his shorts. I wanted to explore his body, touch him, feel him. His loose surf shorts dropped to the floor and he stepped out of them toward me, his erection burning against my belly, pushing me to the edge of the bed.

"Savannah . . ." he sighed, kissing my face and neck, his hands lifting my breasts to fill his mouth. As he nibbled, licked and sucked, electricity shot into my pulsating clitoris. His touch thrilled me. My hungry mouth devoured every place on his body within my reach.

Nudging me onto the bed, lying me down in front of him, he leaned over me and I opened my legs and pulled him close, inviting him into my inner sanctum. He pushed me onto the middle of the bed and to my surprise, spread my labia, leaning in to sample the juicy delicate flesh dedicated to this indulgence. I surrendered to the sensations, thrilled that he so readily found his way to my obvious need. I wanted to taste him too and he sensed my desire. Fluidly turning his body, he maneuvered us into a classic pose designed for erotic oral ecstasy. I filled my mouth with his delicious piece, the taste of him, the sounds of his stifled groans tempting me to suck him deeper into my throat until I reached my threshold. He managed to keep his focus on me and bring me to the edge, then took me over. I moaned and involuntarily released him. He gently pulled away and watched me as I crescendoed.

"Savannah . . . Jesus. Your mouth . . . the way you do that." His voice evaporated into a deep sigh.

"Finn . . . please. Please I need you, I want you inside of me." He leaned over the side of the bed, reaching for his shorts on the floor. From his pocket he produced a condom. Quickly unwrapping it, he slipped it on before slowly entering me. Heaven revealed itself in a glory of streaming light and color when I felt him start to move inside of me. I sensed that he wanted to hold on as he penetrated me more deeply. I couldn't. As another orgasm began to surge from my depths, he held me tightly, molding himself to me as we moved in rapturous harmony. It happened then. He shuddered, groaning, pumping himself into me. I surrendered to him completely.

That Thing! is potent. *That Thing!* is magic. *That Thing!* that intimates and manifests itself in the moment, continued as a slow hot burn in the wake of our passion. We were lost in it. Unwilling to let go of what we had just shared, our bodies were entwined from lips to toes. He tenderly traced the smile on my lips with his finger. I buried my face in his neck. In time we rolled onto our backs, closed our eyes and held hands in fused gratification. What could surpass this pleasure, this auspicious beginning, this beautiful morning?

There would be no going out for breakfast. This was my idea. How could we hide what was occurring with us now? I was certain that I could not, not this morning. *That Thing!* is hypnotic as well as revealing. Other people can also perceive it. When I described my awareness about the nature of That Thing! Finn innately understood and concurred. I convinced him that his friends in this nosey little village would surely take notice. I wanted to protect and preserve our privacy, and of course, so did he. So now what to do? How to spend the day?

"If I had realized I would be lying here next to you, feeling like this, I would have cleared my day," he lamented. "I have several business obligations and, dammit, a dinner tonight with some friends who are coming in from out of town."

I laughed. He turned to me, confused, an expression of concern on his face. When I explained the serendipity of how Milo had pestered me earlier about the party tonight and how I resisted, hoping to be able to spend time with him, we both laughed. Wrapped in each other's arms as we were now, reluctant to let go, intimacy threatened to become an exercise in restraint at the dinner table.

"I might enjoy tormenting you tonight at dinner," I teased. He laughed, but in his expression, I briefly registered alarm. Kissing away his concern, I assured him, "Don't worry. I would never compromise you on purpose. That wouldn't serve either of us well. My only consideration now is enjoying every minute of this week. I hope we can spend as much of it together as humanly possible."

"That should be simple enough to accomplish," he smiled and kissed me lightly all over my face. "There isn't anything I want more now. I'll get these few commitments out of my way today so we can stretch every minute and squeeze every ounce of pleasure out of it."

When we parted, I made some tea, and discovered that Milo had thoughtfully stocked the fridge with fresh fruit, yogurt and some pan dulce for breakfast. Sitting at the little bistro table in the courtyard, I let my thoughts drift over the events of last night and this heavenly morning. Later, after returning from a long walk on the beach and a little shopping, I spent a couple hours sitting there again in the mottled shade of the courtyard, writing. By late afternoon I announced to Fernando that I was not going to be able to sit at a dinner table with a bunch of people and be confident that I could hide my feelings about Finn. Putting either of us to the test, as I had teased him earlier, sounded more stressful than fun. Fernando blinked once and resumed not moving. Just before 6:00, Milo wandered down to the courtyard, saw that I was not ready to go and began a relentless demand for me to get up, get dressed and come with him. "Settle down. You're disturbing Fernando and you're annoying me. I'm in the middle of a creative outburst and don't want to be interrupted."

"Bullshit," he bellowed. "I insist. Get ready. You'll enjoy these people." He's loud even in his quiet moments, and it doesn't take much to rev him up. That and he's used to having his commands obeyed. I'm not intimidated by him.

"Rein it in, Milo. I don't want to go."

"I ran into Finn earlier and he told me how much he was looking forward to seeing you again. I already told him and the others you would be joining us tonight. They'll all be disappointed. Now get dressed."

"Nice try." Milo has never been above using guilt, but this time that tactic and the sly smile he was wearing only served to put me on alert. He already suspects something about Finn's and my budding friendship. Knowing him as I do, I was sure he was going to find ways to embarrass us. My tenacious amigo would not take no for an answer.

"Okay, Milo. I'll get dressed in a minute and meet you at the restaurant when I'm ready." I had no intention of doing so. I also had no way to alert Finn of my desertion plans. I figured when Milo explained my tardiness, and then when I didn't show, he would intuit the reason and I felt confident that he would come to me as soon as he could get away.

I spent the evening titillated, imagining spending the entire night making love, waking up in his arms, preparing breakfast for him. As the hours passed, I could no longer concentrate on writing and began to fret. Midnight arrived, Finn didn't. I was crestfallen and wore myself out with imagined scenarios, self-doubt and recrimination that spilled into my dreams. I spent the night miserable and alone.

I awoke at dawn to him tapping on my bedroom screen. I opened the door for him, raw from a night of such surprising emotional attachment. My eyes betrayed me further and threatened to well up with tears at the sight of him. Unable to hide my emotion, I was equally distressed and thrilled to see him. He took me into his arms, kissing me, his eyes glazed with concern. I was relieved and at the same time aware of his palpable tension. I knew it wasn't about me.

"I had to see you before I leave for the airport," he explained. The airport? He's leaving? "Last night at dinner, the dinner you never showed up for, I received a call telling me that my daughter was hurt in a car accident on her way home from college. She was rushed to the hospital. That's all I know. I can't get through to anyone to see about her condition." I stepped back to observe him more carefully. The stress in his body and worry on his face broke my heart. He explained that he had been able to book a flight early this morning and was on his way now, but couldn't leave before seeing me. "Why didn't you come last night, Savannah? I've been beside myself, worrying about what I have to face at home. That, compounded with unwelcome insecurities about you, made for a wretched night."

"After making love with you and reminiscing about every second of it all day, I didn't think I could sit next to you with Milo and your friends watching us. I was sure I couldn't keep from touching you or at least keep my fire for you from being obvious. I had to tell Milo I was coming even though I knew I wasn't, because he wouldn't take no for an answer. Although I realize I was delusional now, last night I felt so certain you would somehow see through the ruse and come to me after dinner. I wish you had, you could have shared this with me and I could have comforted you. Why didn't you just come to me? I'm sure you can see I made myself miserable all night, as well."

"When you didn't show, I thought maybe I had misread you and maybe you had changed your mind. Milo explained your absence by saying you didn't want to be disturbed from your writing. I took that personally. That fucking dismal idea, on top of the inability to get any news about my daughter has been nothing but a sleepless anxiety. I wanted to be with you, I needed you. I didn't think the feeling was mutual. I thought you had a change of heart." His confession was a relief and his vulnerability a redeeming sweetness to witness. I held him and kissed him tenderly, relieved to learn that we'd merely had a miscommunication and not a disconnect. He collapsed in my arms. All the self-admonishments I tortured myself with through the night melted away. I felt both sad and conflicted. I could only imagine how he felt. I knew if the tables were turned and it were my child injured and I were this far away, I would be undone. I hated the idea of him leaving. I still had a week before my return home and I selfishly wanted to spend every second of it with him, especially now that we'd shared such delicious intimacy.

I didn't intend to elicit *That Thing!* It elicits itself without consent or concern for other plans. As if on cue, our melancholy gave way to searing desire. He ripped off my gown, tearing it across the front to expose my breasts. His mouth devoured my neck and shoulder, I kissed him voraciously. He kicked off his shorts and shoved me back onto the bed and thrust himself into me with such frenzied determination that if we hadn't so lusciously experienced each other only 24 hours before, I would have felt attacked. The force of his immediacy triggered a torrent of emotion in me and I opened to him greedily. We detonated simultaneously.

I dug my nails into his back, drawing blood. He bit me hard on my shoulder as he ejaculated. I screamed, he cursed. I would have bruises, he would have scars to explain. Love bites, scratches and bruises would be the souvenirs from our uncensored passion.

The truth about *That Thing!* is that it doesn't necessarily mean falling in love. It doesn't necessarily mean forever after. I know from experience that it simply happens, suddenly and randomly. The essence of it is a mystery. What becomes of the mutual awareness of such undeniable connection will depend on many factors. When it happens easily, when it all falls into place, when there is no reason not to respond, it is the spice of life. It's a calling to pleasure in the moment whatever the ultimate outcome.

I fully understood that he had to go. I also hated it. Still I am grateful for the gift of connecting with him on this trip to Las Sirenas. We can never know what the future will bring, we can only wish one another well. There is no point in making plans or lamenting about any of that. For us, *That Thing!* was triggered and unleashed and cannot be denied. I don't regret it and I know I won't ever forget, and should the fates allow, we'll meet again.

About The Author

Savannah Aries is a sassy, passionate, contemporary woman who claims and advocates *Pleasure as a Higher Calling*. Her spicy stories of life, love, sensuality and lust highlight the adventures of a juicy mature woman, creating, navigating and enjoying the new rules of engagement.

Women (and men!) of all ages are delighting in her humorous perspective, peppered with a bit of well-deserved angst, as she attempts to unravel and make sense of life's most enduring mystery: the luscious story of Love.

Savannah lives in the beautiful Pacific Northwest.

If you enjoyed *Easy & Delicious*, you'll want to read the other books in the *Pleasure as a Higher Calling* series:

Waking Up

No Regrets

Visit Savannah's Author Website:
www.savannaharies.com

amazon.com/author/www.savannaharies.com

Follow Savannah on social media:
facebook.com/savannah.aries

twitter.com/savannaharies

instagram.com/savannaharies6127

www.ingramcontent.com/pod-product-compliance
Lightning Source LLC
Chambersburg PA
CBHW022041170626
46808CB00003B/1316